The Killing Stroke

Josh Guy Kemp

1

Ironically enough, Gareth found the descriptions of his murders to be more gruesome and drawn out on paper. In reality his victims died quickly, cheating him of the simple pleasure he derived from witnessing their immutable suffering. Gareth did not enjoy the fact that this book was embellishing his story, he decided that he would discuss this with Phillip during their next session.

"Phillip, I am worried that you are misrepresenting my art," Gareth said.

"However do you mean?" Phillip asked.

"For example, you have written that my last victim cried out for help. This description, simply put, would be impossible—I stabbed her with a boning knife. It was cleanly inserted into the lung. Once the lungs begin to fill with blood, an effective scream would become implausible," said Gareth with a glint of trepidation in his eye. "Do you aim to portray me as an amateur Phillip?"

"Why no, my good sir, I would never portray you as an amateur. It only, well, adds to the suspense," Phillip stammered whilst fiddling with a pen in his sofa chair, he continued as if he were speaking to a child. "Do you understand? If her screams go unanswered, then it will speak to the reader...The reader imagines that *they* are the character and how terrified *they* might be if nobody had answered *their* desperate cries for salvation!" Phillip exclaimed, rising from his chair with underwhelming energy.

2

"Phillip, I believe your theory is terrible," Gareth said. "It is far more terrifying for a human to have their lungs filled with blood. Despite their best efforts, they are helpless to interfere with my art. As I approach them and begin to make my incisions, their eyes speak out with great relief. Soon it will be over they think, yet they have no idea that my work has just begun. If only they could scream out for…"

Gareth inched himself closer and closer to Phillip, until he could feel the laborious exhales flee Phillip's lungs. "*Salvation*, do you not find this frightening Phillip?"

"Oh yes! Horrid to say the least, brilliant to say the most! How brilliant it is, to stab a victim in their lungs—in a crowded spot that is filled with people! My dear friend, may I take some creative liberties with the

3

story? Writing that it did indeed take place in a crowded spot? This would immensely help in the efforts to sell your novel! If you agree to this, I will omit the screaming from this victim, and this…"

Phillip pondered for a moment. "I suppose this would suffice in it's place, how does that sound to you?" Phillip asked, sitting, pen in hand.

"You would make her silent, like she was?"

"Why yes, indeed I would,"

Phillip raised a finger high in the air with considerable effort; his age would often bleed through his excitement, "on the condition that you allow me the license to elaborate on the setting, oh, ever so slightly my boy—ever so slightly."

Phillip wagged his finger.

"I performed my art in a stairwell at the Greenwood Estate Inn, near the north side entrance, on the first floor. Where would you have it take place?"

"I'd do nothing too drastic, I'd only change a few names. Perhaps add one, or two men just a few floors above, en route to their hotel room. That's all. Meanwhile you would be below butchering this poor woman, unbeknownst to them."

Phillip grinned a crooked line across his wrinkled jaw.

"That would scare one of them...I worry though, that it makes me look as if I am an amateur—I surveyed for witnesses and the presence of security cameras beforehand. From there I planned my route into the hotel, then I waited for my victim beneath the stairwell—and you have documented the rest. In your new idea, it makes it sound as if I had not surveyed the second, third, and fourth floor several times at intervals. It makes me look like some hatch job killer who hides under stairwells!" Gareth flew from his seat, throwing his arms up in a huff.

"Please understand, this makes for a tense read. It is not to make you look foolish, you will be seen as the opposite in fact, as a killer so bold and confident in his work that he is willing to do it in the presence of others!" Phillip assured him.

"You are correct, they would think this," Gareth said whilst contemplating. "Some may think what I do is grotesque, they do not understand the art. How can murder not be art when they will pay money to watch it on their televisions and in their theatres?" Gareth continued, while pacing and

6

throwing about frantic hand gestures. "In what way am I more perverse than those who enjoy the emulation of my art?" He stopped. "My hope is that one day, through the publication of this novel, I will be respected among the great artists," Gareth finished with a hearty sigh.

"Trust me my boy, you will be hailed as one of the greats among the infamous American killers!" Phillip promised him.

"Do not call me that!" Shouted Gareth.

"Don't call you what?" Phillip shot back in surprise.

"I do not enjoy the term killer, like you said, I am an artist. That is the term I prefer. You would not call a sketch artist a scribbler," Gareth was saying while marching back and forth through Philip's office, he suddenly paused and raised a finger high to make a point. "Remember my terminology when you are writing my book," Gareth pointed at Philip and his finger grew closer to his face with every word. "I do not wish to be misrepresented. I have done a lot of research for you, friend."

Gareth grimaced.

"I would not usually go to such lengths to obtain victims…or parts, for me it's usually quite simple and not as complicated as what you request. In my opinion your desires are cliché Phillip."

"Ah, but cliché is what the audience wants, you give them realism and it's boring. It needs to seem as if there is a message behind what I'm writing, instead of just showcasing grotesque crimes."

"Is that what you think of my art Philip? Grotesque crimes?"

"No! Not at all, that is what *they* think."

"Who?" Gareth inquired, as he sensed Philip's deflection.

"Nobody in particular my boy, that's just the overall view on murder right now, I aim to change that. Change that with our book Gareth! You and me, together we can make them respect you. Respect you akin to the likes of Picasso! How does that sound to you, my boy?" Phillip asked with an answer in mind.

"I would like that," Gareth admitted.

"I know you would, now tell me whatever happened to that poor sap from the other week?" Phillip clicked his pen and began writing.

2

Lethargy coursed through his veins, Chuck awoke with a headache and reached towards his bedside table for a tablet of Aspirin. He couldn't move his right hand; it was bound to his left. Chuck felt warm blood slide down his forehead, something terrible had happened. Something he didn't remember. Upon opening his eyes he found himself tied to a chair, in the middle of an empty warehouse.

"Hello, I am Gareth," Said an unfamiliar voice. Then a man stepped into eye-shot. He was well kempt with hair parted perfectly on either side of his face. This man looked quite sharp, his black tapered pants and sweater-vest suggested so. What on Earth did he want with Chuck Langhorne?

He started to speak.

"I believe you are confused, allow me to help you understand your circumstances. I am going to kill you Chuck. There's nothing you can do or say to change that, I could explain to you why I would be doing so, although I doubt you'd be interested. Most aren't."

"Oh, I'm interested."

"There's no need to lie to me. I am waiting for a call, until that call comes in I cannot kill you. Once I get the call, we can continue. I do apologize for the wait."

"I'm interested!" Spat Chuck.

"You're only saying this because you're about to be killed Chuck. Don't fool yourself, it's really quite boring," Gareth said, as if he were saving him the trouble.

"No, truly! I am interested in your motivation. Yet if you feel that I'm lying, don't tell me anything," Chuck said with ebullition.

"You are correct to call them unique, if you would like to know I suppose we have a minute or two before I am to slaughter you. Very well. You are here for something very special, something you should feel grateful about being involved in. Chuck, you are art! Once I kill you, your story will be one of many in my new book from the soon to be great…Phillip Fairview!" Gareth announced.

"Did you say Fairview?" Chuck asked, wide eyed.

"Yes, Phillip Fairview."

"Phillip Fairview, who runs the writer's circle on 79th?"

"How did you…You know him?"

"Yeah…He's the one who organized the thing a while back, only that we had a problem with attendance and people stopped showing. Now the address and phone number bit of the signup sheet make a little more sense—I think I'm gonna be sick!" Chuck said, and wretched.

"What were their names?" Gareth asked in curiosity.

"I don't want to ask," Chuck said with a quivering voice.

13

"Don't worry—I won't be offended," Gareth assured him.

"It's not that at all," Chuck retorted in amazement at his train of thought.

"I'm going to have you ask now, whatever your reservations are," Gareth said.

"Jennifer Mangrove, Charlie Esposito, Marcus Danelli, Christopher Horwood—" Chuck was saying.

"All of them."

"What do you mean by all of them?"

"I killed all of them, continue."

"I don't…I don't know if I want to do that."

"You will."

"Daniel Haldiman, Tilly Karter, Mason Gibbs…That's all," Chuck sighed.

"I was just discussing Tilly with Phillip earlier today. How very interesting."

"So what? He's like, writing about this? That's sick, Jesus Christ, I even helped him edit some of his work!" Chuck said while straining his hands, tugging at his bonds.

"Oh I see, now that you've realized that his work was based on reality it unsettles you. Interesting, you now deduce an alternate meaning from the same descriptions. Before you probably saw them as genius, yet now you are disgusted. You humans are interesting creatures."

"I didn't know real people were dying! Otherwise I'd have never helped in the first place!" Chuck shouted in his defense.

"That is where you draw the issue? Because it is real? I have a query for you Chuck. Have you ever watched a *true crime* show?"

"Well yes, I must have seen one before, they're always on television."

"Okay. Now think of this, those people who make *true crime* shows line their pockets while creating entertainment from real life murders. I am sure that fact did not give you any reservations about consuming the media. I doubt you would stop yourself from going to the theater and watching a movie that was *based on a true story*. In fact it makes you people run out to the theater all the more if you know it happened to someone, somewhere. Here is my point Chuck, nobody cares where their consumerist products come from. Be it in the form of entertainment or the leather wallet that you have been carrying. Nobody cares if someone had actually been murdered in order for such a picture to be made. They purchased a ticket *because* someone was actually murdered. People like it when it is true. They think that since it has already happened there is no hurt in relishing in the details. They are wrong, they pay for front row seats to the bloody action and demand more. Then they are shocked when it happens again! I am sure you seldom think of how many corpses make your simple life possible. Because you don't care, nobody does! It is the same attitude you carry towards animals. Since you are not murdering them yourselves, that makes it okay for you to buy your leather wallet from someone who will kill for you! Since you are not doing the murder yourself you think it makes you somewhat better,"

17

Gareth said, as if he were a parent teaching his child manners. "This is not true, if a man pays for another man to be a murdered—you would call him a murderer. Yet a man who pays for an animal to be killed you do not call a murderer. What are you then? None of you do the hard work, you sit back and let others get their hands filthy with the viscous fluids while you sit on your couch and watch what some buffoon has to say about another man's art. Meanwhile, the only man who could truly explain it is locked behind bars! What a joke, what an absolute joke that is! At the same time you pay the man who reports on the *crime*, that is what I call art theft! Plagiarists!" Gareth fumed and clenched his fists as he spoke. "They always take murder stories from local artists and nobody cares. You sit on your couches and fork steak into your mouth without even thinking about the *murderer* who brought it to you. What you forget is that you are buying more than steak at the store, you are buying a clear conscience. Is that not one of the most bought and sold items in the world? You people make murderers famous! Yet here you are trying to shame me in an attempt to reach for my dreams," Gareth scoffed, suddenly his back pocket began vibrating.

"Please excuse me for a moment," Gareth said, suddenly disappearing behind Chuck's field of view.

He began hearing what sounded like Gareth talking on the phone.

"Hello Phillip.

Why yes, I have him right here.

Do you think so?

19

It is quite impractical, although it can be done.

I suppose I may.

Have you considered my suggestions?

I believe you should, I am the expert after all

Philip.

You said this yourself.

I understand, I await our next visit."

Gareth finished and tucked the phone back into his pocket, his footsteps sounded far louder from behind and Chuck feared a blade would be tucked into the back of his neck. Chuck expelled a tense breath when Gareth stepped in front of him once more, with his hands folded in his lap as if he was about to deliver bad news to someone of infantile composure.

"Phillip has asked that I remove your innards whilst you are still breathing. How does this sound?"

Gareth asked in a soothing voice, having the opposite desired effect.

"May I say something?" Chuck asked, his anxiety shattering his confident facade.

"Do not object please."

"I don't object, instead I have a suggestion, how does that sound?"

"I am listening, be quick."

"Instead of tearing out my entrails while I live, instead I believe you should…Cut off my head with a hatchet!" Chuck shouted, feigning excitement.

"Why? What game are you playing?"

"No games, for I am a writer too. Just like Phillip, I believe in this type of creative project you've been conducting. While I must admit that at first I was jarred, I am slowly becoming used to the idea. Your speech has enlightened me so!"

"I will not lie—I am intrigued by this idea. Although Phillip would never allow me to perform my art in a way that is contrary to his liking," Gareth told him while he fetched his hatchet.

"Why do you listen to Phillip at all? It seems you are doing all the work, as you said yourself, why should he profit when you do all the hard work?" Chuck instigated while anxiously wriggling.

Gareth ran his finger along the blade of the hatchet—drawing a minute drop of blood, he looked into the droplet as if he were pondering as it slid down his finger and onto the concrete floor beneath him.

"I would not want to go against Phillip, he has taken my art a long way after all. He seeks to publish my work, turning me into a great American artist!" Gareth boasted, throwing his arms up in triumph.

"I too could do the same Gareth," Chuck said with nonchalance.

"What reason would I have to choose yourself over the masterful Phillip?" Gareth asked, pointing the hatchet in Chuck's direction.

"I am also a writer, in fact I'm better than Phillip. I've published three of my own works, all critically acclaimed!" Chuck received no reaction, so he decided to change the subject. "Before, when folks would leave the circle, we assumed they got too good for our little group and went off to California or wherever they think successful authors go…Now, well, now I know…"

"May I share something with you?" Gareth asked suddenly.

"Why, yes," Chuck said, feeling comfortable with his current position.

"I believe Phillip is misrepresenting me in his writing. I offer him suggestions, although more often than not, he discards my input and thoroughly offends me."

"Have you tried talking to him about it?" Chuck asked.

"That would be no use. Phillip I believe, does not respect murder as an art."

"With all you've already done, I could make a best seller for you. Nobody cares about the victims today, it's all about the perpetrator. Truly, I can see you becoming something of a blockbuster hit after

24

releasing your book, the public won't care what you've done, as long as it interests them. If you kill me though, unfortunately my fingers could not type," Chuck said while shrugging, as if to suggest he would consent to the murder otherwise.

"You're very right Chuck! I will tell him tomorrow; I will turn to him and say—!" In a quick turning motion Gareth swung to face Chuck, forgetting the hatchet in his hand.

It collided into Chuck's head with a thunk, shattering his skull.

In shock, Gareth released his grasp on the hatchet. Chuck's head fell limply against his chest, blood pouring from the broken canyon between his eyes. Gareth held his breath whilst pacing back and forth. He would do so until a significant puddle had gathered around the chair in which Chuck's body sat.

Gareth paced through the blood as if he did not notice

that he was splattering it onto his clothing with the

kicks of his feet. Gareth abruptly began jumping

around and shouting, throwing a proper fit. Tossing

himself around in the blood and flipping over the chair

in which Chuck had sat, then his phone began to ring.

He stood up and straightened his composure before

answering, he gingerly fished the phone out of his

pocket with two fingers so as to not lather it in blood.

"Hello Phillip."

"Gareth, I just wanted to check in to make sure

everything was going alright."

"I told you not to call me whilst I'm working."

"Ah, I'm aware of your rule but I have good

news!"

"Okay." Gareth said in monotone.

"We've secured a publisher—he loves the idea and is very excited to present it to an American audience!"

"That is…Good work Phillip," Gareth said and gazed towards Chuck's body, as if his limp corpse was just a mess that needed to be cleaned up. "May I call you back later?"

"Why yes of course my boy…May I ask why?"

"No you may not. Goodbye Phillip," Gareth tucked the phone back into his pants pocket, then he fetched a mop.

3

"Hello all, on behalf of the rest of the group—I'd like to welcome you newcomers to The Writer's Circle!" Phillip exclaimed while surveying today's participants.

His regulars nodded in agreement and some gave faint claps.

"You know, when I first came up with the idea to form The Writers Circle, I ran into some obstacles. How could I snare people in? What would make someone want to share something so sacred with a group of people?" Phillip paced around the circle of people waiting for a response that would not come. "Why the love of writing of course! I didn't always know this. I arranged the first meeting and then over time I began to find the right people to include. I've had many amazing writers come and go in since the first time we gathered," Phillip huffed proudly. "Those of you who remain are the best," The words almost choked him, although the writers were convinced and clapped loudly for Phillip's praise.

A wry smile crawled across his face.

"So let's have you start us off Becky, we'll begin with discussing what we thought of Ryan's story." Phillip gestured to Becky, prompting her to speak.

"Okay so, in Ryan's story I really liked how the main character actually became exactly what hurt him in the first place. He ends up becoming an echo of all the pain and suffering that he had to go through. To me that was really interesting," Becky said.

"So you think that this was a negative thing for the protagonist?" Phillip asked.

"Well yeah, if you *really* look at what's being said you can see that he's so broken that he doesn't question what he's becoming and that was really powerful."

"I had another interpretation, if I may?" Phillip asked, as if her opinion somehow restricted his own.

"Go ahead, I'd like to hear it."

"In my mind, Ryan's character—or Darren had taken on the strong attributes of those who had wronged him and became all that they couldn't. He succeeded in the ways that they failed. An amazing story of triumph!" Phillip huffed, the class all made notes and nodded agreeably.

"But didn't you see how the character was suffering? He achieved all these great things on the outside, but on the inside not so much, his big house might as well have been derelict for all it mattered. He profited from being foul and it made him foul," Becky said.

"I have to say, Beckys right. That's what I meant when I initially wrote it—but after you finish your work, I think it sort of takes on a life of it's own. There's no right answer, I like both your ideas," Ryan said.

"Just quickly, another thing—why is it that writers always find some way to write about writers?" Becky asked. "I mean do we have such huge egos that the most interesting thing we can seem to write about are writers? Do we think that our craft is so interesting

31

that all others are dwarfed by it? Or rather do we just

write from experience and other crafts are out of our

realm, if so—then are we truly *great* writers?"

Ryan was amazed by her insight—and if he

was being honest, it made him want to throw his whole

story out. Though he wouldn't tell her that. He was

about to say something but Phillip cut him off.

"Now Becky, you were saying something

about how the characters were *poorly* presented in

Ryan's work?" Phillip asked as he ran his hands

through his mockery of a beard.

"Well, I just thought—not that it's anything

bad…But he might want to edit it so that we—the

reader, know who's talking when…and well, to make

the dialogue sound like how real people actually talk. It

sounds a little too much like—well, like it's written.

Sorry," Becky trailed off hesitantly while Ryan meticulously made notes in his pocket journal.

"There's no need to be sorry in the writer's circle. This is a place of well-being and friendship, we only knock our fellow writers because we care about what happens to them. We wouldn't want someone to produce something less than their absolute best! Critique is a compliment—it means the person gives a damn enough to offer their wisdom on how you might take your ideas further. It means you see potential in them, Becky. *Sorry*. I never want to hear that word here again. In fact, it's banned!" Phillip laughed as if he were making a coy joke, although he was completely serious in his assertion.

Everyone made note of this in their pocket journals. He never did want to hear anyone apologize again. He found it incredibly weak minded to offer up

something for which you would immediately

apologize. Perhaps he would add her to the list.

4

Another corpse lay lifeless on the metallic workbench while Gareth sharpened his tools, he snapped on his latex gloves and adjusted the radio to exhume his favorite tune whilst he worked his art. Meticulous chords began to flood his ears and he began dissection. Pressing the knife blade against the skin, Gareth tore back what used to be a face and placed it on the tray to his left facing downwards; he found it awfully creepy if the face was looking at you. Gareth would remove the eyes from the sockets and place them into a dish to his right. He liked to separate the parts from the skins, it was more organized that way. Tearing back the chest, he found all the interestingly shaped organs he was looking for. Gareth rolled up the skin that he removed from the chest and deposited that carefully into the tray to his left. Gareth took a moment to find his boning knife and adjusted the volume of the music, its ghostly vocals pleased him. He used the boning knife to separate those tricky bones from his subject's flesh. It worked like a charm; he had become masterful at this part. He should have liked to save the skull but it was terribly mashed in, unfortunately he was forced to sever its connection from the rest of the work. Into the bucket at his feet it went with a thud, then a loud sloshing sound floated into his ears as the residual blood soaked out of the thing. This subject had good rib bones, he could use these for another one of his sculptures. They were truly spectacular pieces. Unfortunately he couldn't use any of the internal parts for sculptures. Instead he kept them for a time, admiring their composition, only to later see them wither and rot. To Gareth, they were like his flowers. He kept them in water and they decorated his home. Skin on the other hand could be preserved in many ways and that was why he adored the process of collecting it, he thought about using this specimen to

wrap his book once it was published.

5

Lying back on the cushiony velvet, Gareth had decided he would reveal his doubts to Phillip this time. He would do this while Phillip jotted down his account of this week's murders.

"Phillip."

"Yes, m'boy?" Phillip said while intensely documenting what Gareth had just told him. Once he had finished jotting down his last thought, his head sprung up—as if out of a gopher's hole.

"May I read what you have so far?" Gareth asked, extending his hand.

"I don't think I should allow that; it is too far unfinished and would not make sense to a mind as put together as your own," Phillip explained as he folded Gareth's hand back into a fist, placing it on his lap.

"Whatever you are meaning to say Phillip, I can assure you, you are not saying it," Gareth said, sitting himself upright.

"If only you would give me a week more, I'd be happy to share the entire project with you, then you can make the changes as you see fit, how does that sound m'boy?" Phillip held his breath.

"No."

"What do you mean no?" Philip said quizzically, whilst his eyebrow jumped like a startled feline.

"I ask that you show it to me now, I insist upon it," Gareth said.

"If you insist, I will have to desist. I cannot show it to you today, Gareth, do you not trust in my abilities? Have any of your subjects perhaps…" Phillip's face grew cold like a stone, calculations churned through his head. "Have they said anything to you?" Phillip asked, putting the puzzle together.

39

"They say many things."

"What sort of things Gareth?"

"They beg for their lives *Phillip*."

"Anything else?"

"There was the one from earlier this week, Chuck," Gareth said with piercing eyes. "He was *very* talkative."

"Say anything worth noting?" Phillip tried to ask with nonchalance.

"He told me that I should tell you to follow my vision in a way that is closer to my liking."

"That's all?" Philip asked and almost chortled in doing so, there was much more the man could have said.

"Yes that was all. Chuck also gave me a suggestion, one I took in stride." Gareth's tone now became nervous, like a boy who'd spilled milk on the carpet and was afraid to say so. "Now I will reveal to you that I did not disembowel him as you requested, instead I took a hatchet and severed his head. I am now prepared to describe that for you, if you would like. Chuck was very good at making creative choices Phillip," Gareth began to say; Phillip's face grew red with contention.

"Chuck had nothing to offer you, believe me there. I've read all of his manuscripts, infantile in their stylistic choices, every last page of them! Forget he ever existed and grind his bones into dust!" Phillip exclaimed, slamming his fist against his notepad.

"Phillip, you know that I make use of all my parts; I try to let nothing go to waste."

"I know my boy, sometimes I allow my emotions to get the better of me, a flaw of many great writers. Take Ernest Hemingway for example! Anger seems to flow through us writers like a stream that runs on forever," Phillip said.

"You did not tell me of the writer's circle," Gareth said, framing an accusation.

"Oh, it must have simply slipped my mind." Phillip poured himself another drink from the decanter beside him. "I've been rather focused on doing you justice m'boy." Phillip sipped back a pinch of his whiskey and his lips scrunched up like a cat's ass. "Far too focused on getting the story right to think of those simpleminded writers in my circle."

"Lately you have not given me a wide variety of kills. For this I am disappointed in you, they have all been writers. What good is that? I now only have those experiences to draw from, as do you," Gareth anxiously spilled out. "This will negatively impact the book Phillip."

"You, m'boy are incorrect. Writers, they are-how do I say this? Expressive, they know emotion. Better yet, they know how to show it!" Phillip tore out a page of his notebook with an old man's aggression to prove his point. Gareth looked confused by this but Phillip continued on anyway. "They draw from within, they've learned what makes people tick. Once they know how to do that, they make the reader happy and sad. They make the reader laugh and cry, they even frighten them to their core. That is the goal of an author, to sell an experience. That's what we're here to do. I'm going to portray you as the most magnificent anti-hero to ever grace the vanilla pages of a novel. You're going to be relatable to the audience. They shall think that since you have things in common with them you must not be evil, perhaps you just *lost your way*. You will tear them apart with how much they love you, it will eat them up and cause them to miss out on sleep. Only then shall you be cemented as one of the greatest artists of this century. So, the reason I use authors is because they will show you those emotions. Emotions sell, the author who makes the reader feel, he sells his work, handsomely. I would never steer you in the wrong direction. I want only the most intelligent specimens to meet your knife blade. It is the closest intellect we can get without putting my own neck on the chopping block, only then we'd have nobody to write the damn book!" Philip burst into uproarious laughter.

Gareth did not discount his idea, he was right. Nobody else would be able to write his novel other than Phillip. Not anymore.

"Very well Philip, I understand," Gareth said.

"That is excellent my boy, I knew you would. Now please go home and get yourself some rest, you'll need it. I'll have a whole new list for you tomorrow! This is all very exciting! I have much work to complete though, as you'd like to read the first draft sooner than I expected," Phillip said, his intone indicated that Gareth should leave, although Gareth sat still, staring at Phillip with glazed eyes and a look you might see a crocodile give a swallow.

"Phillip, do you believe your work to be hard?" Gareth asked, leading the conversation.

"M'boy every writer believes their work to be hard, they enjoy reaping the benefits of the final product but hate the work necessary for that to become reality. It's quite awful that I can't think my books into existence, you would have an entire series by now!"

"Philip, your work is not hard. What I do is challenging, you are not so talented when compared to myself. You are a secondhand writer, you only relay what I tell you. And you do not do it well. Would I not fair better working on my own?"

"Chuck must have seriously twisted your mind! He is truly an awful specimen; I should have slit his damn throat myself! Gareth you are not a writer, you could not possibly achieve what I do. You may think you can but it takes training, what you say to me is just the basis of the story. Do you think murdering folks is a story on it's own? No I lay out why the reader should care about you at all, I add descriptive elements that you could not fathom!" Phillip argued.

45

"You should be careful how you regard me, Phillip," Gareth warned him.

Phillip's face suddenly grew pale.

"I am sorry my friend, I believe we've both gotten ourselves far too worked up tonight, for that I apologize. Don't take it too personally my friend. I apologize. Let's bury the hatchet, I will adjust the story to your needs," Phillip said.

"That's all I ask Phillip, sleep well." Gareth got up and left.

"No good. All of it, no good, no good at all. Once he lays eyes on these pages the boy will go ballistic, I'll have to move, he'll surely fix his sights on me, I simply cannot give it to him" Phillip said out loud to himself. He pulled the pipe from his mouth and had set it on the oakwood table in front of him, taking a moment to ponder.

"What if…no…perhaps I could…no…aha! Surely I could…well probably not," He kept muttering things to himself, unaware of the solution he felt was just beyond his grasp.

"I'll write another copy of the book! One that would please even a deranged killer! Oh what a marvellous idea, this could be such an excellent writing exercise!" Phillip fished out of his pocket a small recording device. He set it on the table in front of him and hit record, then he began to pace and spew his ideas for the faux novel. One idea he had was that Gareth was an anti-hero sort of killer, Gareth wouldn't like that though. Another would have Gareth as an aspiring artist turned down by the academia and pushed into a life of murder and mayhem. No, that was far too typical. Gareth wouldn't like that either. Phillip did away with all the thinking, he knew what Gareth wanted and he'd write just that. He'd save all the good brainstorming for himself, after all he was giving Gareth a false novel. This was never to be published, the one he wrote could be far greater in comparison. Better yet, he'd never have to show it to the boy, plus by the time it was on shelves Gareth wouldn't be a problem. Phillip grasped his tea and gulped down a hefty swig, in his stomach brewed a tempest.

7

Here they were, the writer's circle had assembled again. Every Sunday they would gather in the library. About half an hour had passed since the group was to begin sharing their stories with one another, Phillip had yet to show up and it was very unlike him. Everyone patiently awaited his arrival, but it didn't seem like he was coming. Just when people were ready to start packing up an old muscle car whipped into the parking lot, it abruptly came to a stop and a man promptly made his way inside. The writers turned to see who the person was, they hoped Phillip had arrived and they could begin sharing their stories.

It was not Philip.

This man looked like a businessman who had just shed his suit after a hard day's work and now carried an unruly look, his shirt sleeves were curled and bent, his eyes were focused.

Gareth made his way to the center of the circle and unsure of where to put it, he set a binder full of paper at his feet.

"Hi—Hello, I will be the replacement for today. When would you like to start?" Gareth asked.

"Where's Phillip today?" Becky asked.

"He is…He is sick. He told me to tell you, he is very sick."

"Do you know when he'll be back?" Ryan asked.

"Soon—he will be back soon." Gareth began to set out some of his papers on the floor, shuffling through them, reorganizing and scanning over the documents. Soon enough the entire class began to wonder what he was doing. Gareth looked up at them gawking and was confused, as if he had woken up in a place unfamiliar to him.

"Go look at each other's work, tell them how brilliant and amazing you found their writing. Even the bad writers, you will tell them their work is good. Phillip told me this is the way it works, get on with it now," Gareth said with a tone that one might use while shooing an insect.

"Which one of you considers yourself the best writer?" Gareth asked, standing up with his hands full of organized papers.

"We don't really do things that way here," Ryan began to say.

"I'm sorry, I don't care how you do things. I am trying to find the best of you, do a vote if you cannot decide but decide, soon."

"The new guy is harsh," Becky whispered to Ryan while laughing, Gareth's gaze sprung at Becky and she quieted her voice at once. Ryan put up his hand and waited to be called on.

"Are you trying to say something to me?" Gareth said after a while.

"Yeah, we've um, decided on who's the best. Phillip usually has us put up our hands before we talk," Ryan said.

Gareth thought of him as a suck up and from that point on he hated Ryan.

"I know it is not you, so who is it?" Gareth asked.

"We all would have picked Chuck but he's been a no show for a bit so they decided that it was Becky but I thought Derek was a bit more experienced because—" Ryan began to say.

"I don't care what you think, I care what they think and they think Becky is better," Gareth told him.

"What did you want me for exactly?" Becky asked.

"I will be working with the best today, the rest of you can share notes and you can all go home whenever you please," Gareth said, leading Becky to a table away from the group. He set his binder full of paper on the table in front of them. Becky turned her head to Ryan and mimed 'help me' to him as a joke. Gareth opened his binder at the table and flipped to the first document, he placed it in front of Becky and waited.

"Did you? You wanted me to read this?" Becky asked.

"Yes," Gareth said, folding his hands upon his lap.

"Like, all of it?" Becky asked.

"Yes, do it now. I'll wait, be quick," Gareth said.

Becky exhaled with pre-exhaustion and began flipping through the mucked-up pages, there were tears in the corner of each and every piece of paper. Some had been crumpled and uncrumpled, ripped and taped back together. Interestingly enough, it was interesting.

Becky found herself unable to put down the work, she was intrigued by the characters, the description, the scene, the setting. It was all so…Horrifying. When she finished, her expectation of exhaustion had turned into a reality of excitement and admiration for the work.

"Gareth is it?" Becky asked, unexpectedly he seemed timid and worried at her feedback as she spoke.

"Yes, how was it?"

"I actually really enjoyed it. Did you write this all yourself?" Becky asked in awe.

"Well yes, me and Phillip have collaborated before but this was purely a solo project," Gareth said, suddenly proud of himself and his accomplishment.

"Well, it's very good. I think you should try and get it published."

"Thank you for your advice, tell Ryan, next time I'll deal with him," Gareth said, packing up his papers.

"You're leaving, already? We usually run for another half an hour at least!" Becky said, surprised.

"I've got all I needed today, anyways I really should be going, I have a lot of work to do at home," Gareth said whilst packing away his last bits of paper. Once finished, like a straight arrow he glided through the front door. He left as quickly as he came. Gareth turned his key and the moment his engine started chugging he exploded back out of the parking lot. He seemed to do this all without looking, he must be an excellent driver as well Becky thought. She returned to the rest of the group to talk with Ryan and let him know he'd get to work with Gareth next time, she found him much more knowledgeable than Phillip. Maybe he was a bit unorthodox and harsh but he said everything plainly and how it was. Ryan was sulking to the rest of the group when she interceded.

"Oh, the golden child is back," Ryan quipped trying to attempt a playful jab, although he was unintentionally revealing his passive aggressive nature behind it, Becky could tell.

"You ought to be nicer ya know, I was coming to tell you he wanted to work with you during our next session. You could learn a thing or two from him," Becky said in stride.

"So I take it you got along with the weirdo just fine? I don't know where Phillip found him but if it keeps on like this I'm not coming back, I don't care if he wants to work with me or not. I don't even care if he thinks I'm better than Tolkien! He's rude and I don't have to put up with it. I'm telling Phillip about this when he's back, mark my words," Ryan ranted on.

"You're really insufferable. You know-you haven't proven that our new group leader is a jerk, you've proven that you're a jerk," Becky said, leaving.

Mouths began to run agape, nobody left the writer's circle early. It was considered extremely rude and unprofessional among the group. Although based on the way Ryan had acted, along with the absence of Phillip others began to vacate their seats as well.

On the other side of the city Phillip sat alone in his study, wrapped as tightly as his arthritic fingers could clutch the fabrics to his body. He shook, his stomach did not agree with him and his bones felt bruised and broken. He was as weak as a matchstick, as hot as one too. Shakily he rattled loose three pills from a painkiller bottle he acquired long ago for his wisdom teeth, popping them into his gullet he found himself his release. Easing away into a painful sleep he forgot about the suffering and the freezing feeling in his spine, he would not wake up in the morning.

8

After the meeting Ryan made his way back home, he was quite annoyed at how all the other writers were acting like he was the one who was off base. He didn't like this new guy one bit, he especially didn't like how he wanted to work alone with Becky. Ryan felt that he was just as good of a writer as she was but nobody respected him. It was completely unfair, Phillip was hard enough on his writing and then comes this Gareth guy who treats him like he should pack up and leave.

'I don't have to put up with this,' Ryan thought, in fact he didn't plan to go to another meeting again.

At least not until Phillip was back.

Anyways he had his own writing to focus on. Unlocking the door, he was excited to begin typing up his story. Flicking on the lights—he saw the vague figure of a man, sitting in *his* writing chair. Who the hell was that and why was he in Ryan's house? Ryan squinted but he couldn't make the man out quite well. Ryan wasn't wearing his glasses, he thought they made him look like a nerd.

"Finally, you're home. The food you keep is awful and your flowers are withering, you should take care of them like I do," Gareth said.

"How the hell did you get in my house!" Ryan shouted.

"Now is not the time for particulars," Gareth said, rising from the seat.

"Ok, I'm gonna have to ask you to leave. Right now buddy!" Ryan said with a put on deep voice. Ryan's veins seemed to jump to the edge of their seats as Gareth made his way up to Ryan. He was testing the water, how close could he get to the man? Ryan was afraid, that was for sure. Would he get physical?

Gareth thought not, he was right. Gareth looked at Ryan, about an inch away from his face.

"You are about to become a part of something much bigger than yourself. This is the only chance you'll ever have to be involved in great writing," Gareth told Ryan who had begun to step backwards away from him. Ryan slipped up on the carpet behind him but Gareth seized his arm before he fell.

"Careful. You might get hurt," Gareth said, drawing a blade from his pocket. "Like this." Gareth pressed the blade to one of Ryan's fingers and began to cut.

"What are you doing!" Ryan screamed, trying to pull free his arm.

"Hold still, you'll make the cut jagged."

"Let go!"

"Okay," Gareth said as his blade made its way through the bone. The finger came loose and Ryan fell over as he was let go of. Gareth smiled as he dangled

the finger above Ryan's head. Ryan fainted.

9

"Wakey wakey sleepy head!" Gareth shouted while jabbing at Ryan's head with a fire poker. Eyes springing open, Ryan saw Gareth and thrusted himself away from him. This flipped the chair he was tied to on its backside. While writhing on the ground Ryan tried to tug at his restraints but the nubs that were once his fingers just moved around aimlessly. He no longer had any fingers on either hand. Ryan was seething in pain as his thick blood slid from his marred hands, he strained against his restraints to no avail. Gareth waited patiently until Ryan was finished with his fit.

"Why can't I feel anything?" Ryan asked in a panic.

"I have gotten my hands on a collection of numbing agents and a good selection of morphine," Gareth explained.

"So you have some sort of mercy…Is that it?" Ryan inquired.

"Not at all, I only use these things so that I can get coherent responses from my subjects. I have discovered that when you dismember humans they experience pain. They find this unbearable and eventually panic, flailing until they eventually die. In other words, think of it as an antidote to *most* of your pain, so that we can talk."

"Talk about what? Why the hell are you doing this? I thought you were one of the writers!" Ryan shouted, confused.

Well, I hope to be—someday. Although currently, I am in some ways what you would refer to as a hunter," Gareth said, examining a selection of knives.

"You don't hunt people!" Ryan exclaimed.

"What is so wrong with hunting a Human? You hunt animals, butcher them like they are nothing.

63

You Humans are truly extraordinary creatures, the first to inherit intelligence, the first to claim superiority." Gareth said, his mouth agape and his breath escaping in a hearty exhale.

"Just because you don't wanna be Human doesn't make you not one. Preach all you want about humans eating meat, we don't torture them like this. Your hypocritical scales of justice don't exonerate you, you're just a maniac who thinks he's different."

"Funny that you think humans don't torture animals. I know you believe you are different as well. You writers label common emotions with uncommon words and expect praise. Do not think I am fooled, you are not special. People like myself are special and people like you wish that you had the guts to do what I do. When I am finished what I am working on all those like me will come from hiding. If your life was not destined to be cut short you would see a new generation of repressed artists come forth."

"All you are is a stunt in evolution. In order to achieve gratification, you kill others, this is probably because you were never able to get that gratification the right way. Some people know better, you don't, you can't. I don't blame you for it, I can't get inside your head and figure you out but if you do have free will and you're not a victim to the workings of your own mind…Well, then you are truly lost. I believe everybody has access to free will, others just start with less. Someday I hope we find a cure for people with your affliction. I really do," Ryan said, examining the ruptured tips of his stump fingers.

Then he took but a single moment to relish in the fact he was alive, he also did this to digest the fact that he was treading on very thin ice with a serial killer and that soon, he might break it.

"I am not sick!" Gareth was shouting, infuriated by Ryan's claims. Pacing to and fro, Gareth had begun to salivate heavily, panting and shouting at the top of his lungs like a child denied a toy. Gareth was screaming that he was not mad, shattering many of Ryan's belongings throughout the house—soon his eye caught delicate china, which Gareth sought to remove from their shelves. Now he proceeded to carry a stack of plates back to Ryan in his chair. Ryan could only hear the clanging of the dishes sliding between one another as they made their way to him, his eyes remained closed.

Suddenly his eyes sprang open as a plate struck him in the chin.

"You have no respect for your superior man, you are akin to a peasant spitting on the shoes of royalty. You are a disgrace to those above you and *you* are truly the sick fool," Gareth spat out at Ryan, throwing another plate and gashing his cheek bone. "Nothing to say? Go on, rub your wounds. Assess the damage...Oh! But you can not, it seems my memory fails me nowadays. Well with my sickness and all,"

Gareth said, whilst remaining very pleased with himself. Ryan bled, coughing through his words while he tried to speak.

"When you kill, you cut—corners. Cutting corners is a mistake, nature thrives off of mistakes. An animal that forgets to crawl back into its burrow before sleeping gets devoured. You'll be devoured, wither and rot, you and those like you. You're all cowards," Blood dripped from Ryan's mouth as he spoke.

"Cowards! You do not have the right to that opinion! You are sitting there tied to a chair, meanwhile you forget that this is not a philosophy class. As if you can determine morality at the drop of a pen!" Gareth shouted while Ryan struggled to keep his head up.

"Your logic is flawed, morality is not up for debate, as many would like to argue. It has never been a question; everyone likes to pretend it is a question to justify their actions as if righteousness is an opinion.

67

No one man can change the world, but many men, all alike will eventually do it. No matter how many of you evil sick maniacs come in the way of us. Do what you're gonna do and get on with it," Ryan said finally with his last effort.

Ding dong. Somebody was at the door, Ryan sighed a breath of relief, maybe he would get out of this after all. It's funny that way, the universe, one moment you're preparing for death, the next you're home free.

"Is that the door now Ryan?" Gareth asked rhetorically.

"Hey, Ryan…Um, It's me Becky, I—uh wanted to say that I think we should talk. I don't like how things ended last time we saw each other and we've been friends forever and well, I mean I wanna work things out." Ryan's blood ran cold, this was the only time where he didn't want her help, things could go terrible for her very quickly.

"Should I let her in? The three of us can have a little chat, no?" Gareth was saying.

"Don't touch her, I swear to—"

"What will you do? Take my knife with all of your fingers and stab me through the heart? You will do nothing. Sit there like a good pet and watch the show," Gareth told him.

"Becky, go home! Get the fuck out of here now!" Ryan shouted in plea.

"Come on, don't be ridiculous, we can work it out," Becky said.

"No it's not like that, run, Becky you need to run! Now!" Ryan shouted.

"Don't worry, I'll be there in a jiffy!" Gareth said in a low tone, concealing his voice as he galloped over to the door, opening it slightly ajar to greet Becky.

"Oh hi, Gareth? Are you working with Ryan?" Becky asked.

"Something like that." Gareth pulled out his knife and drove it into Becky's neck, digging into her collar bone and dragging her inside, dead and limp, like a lion tossing a ravaged gazelle to the ground.

"Look at her, Look at her! This is your doing. I did not want to do this, in fact I quite liked her, she was not all that difficult. Though I had to show you this," Gareth said in a tone you might find from a father who had killed his son's dog to prove a point, that life was harsh and unforgiving.

After brutally slaying one of Ryan's closest friends, he began to pace around the corpse and inspect it's curious details. Ryan pulled against his restraints in seething rage, Gareth found him silly and dramatic.

"Look at you, struggling when you know it is useless. Is this display just for show? You melodramatic boy. Your emotions get the better of you, for me I do not have such a problem, you say my evolution is stunted yet here I am unfazed by this non-

70

issue. You on the other hand are seething with rage, attempting the impossible. I fear the fingerless man who wishes to strangle me, they might write a ballad in your honor." Gareth laughed loudly.

"You sick bastard, you people will never know the extent of the feelings I felt when I was with her, the two of us worked together to perfect a craft, to touch people's lives. We wanted to make this world a little less dark, a little less like you sick bastards!"

"Ah! But what happened to your little theory now? Truly, the worms will flourish off of the corpses my people make of you weak sheep, in the den of wolves."

"Killing doesn't make you superior, there's always a better man, a stronger man, for the strongest man can be beaten by mere circumstance. You've been testing the laws of nature for some time now I imagine, each time you've gotten away with killing but your time will come and you'll pay for this, you'll pay for her, just know whatever is in store for you, remember it's from us," Ryan said.

"You sentimental fools, inventing laws of nature to attack your enemies in order to seek some sort of relief from the unfairness of reality. You will never see your justice, nor will the rest of the world, nor does it matter what happens after you are dead," Gareth said.

"No, it's not the universe who will repay you, it's yourself. Your story is already written by the choices you've made. It won't matter what happens when I die, not to me. If I was you though, I'd be worried," Ryan said.

"Your stupid beliefs will be your undoing, or I will be, more accurately." Gareth smirked to himself, never before did he actually enjoy the process of killing.

Before he just saw it as a means necessary to complete his artwork.

He had never met somebody who infuriated him as much as Ryan had.

"Forget about all that nonsense, you are only spewing your superstitions and beliefs to give your death some sort of meaning, it is the last thing you have control over before I make you spill your guts. Literally. I do not blame you, perhaps in the same situation I might do something similar, but I am not in that situation. It is you who will die, not in millions of years through the culling of those who share your personality but here and now. You will be killed in this house, the one you own, the one I occupy. I want you to understand this because for all intents and purposes the only thing that should matter to your little brain is the here and now. And now you will feel pain unlike anything you have ever felt before in your life. Your morphine should be wearing off in about ten minutes, yet I am not sure how long your adrenaline will last you. Although I should leave you now. I need to be up

73

bright and early tomorrow morning to run my writer's circle!" With that Gareth strode out of Ryan's house.

Tied to the chair Ryan began to experience a slight discomfort and pressure in his fingers, soon he would be screaming in excruciating pain.

10

Their meeting was in session, Gareth folded his hands across his lap and thoughtfully began the class. He had purchased glasses at the store which he was now wearing, he thought they made him seem more like Phillip.

More sophisticated, he thought.

Gareth eyed his specimens, his students rather.

"Good morning to you. I expect you are all still uncommon with myself, I am aware that my methods may seem unorthodox but I assure you I am seasoned in the craft. I have closely worked with Philip for many years and he has learned much of what he has taught you from me. I too could teach you those secrets of the trade. Perhaps today you will find out something you didn't know, something you might not believe. In fact, I will tell you that with Phillip I have been working on a biography concerning my own exploits, today I may seek to share with you these bodies of work and see if you can improve upon them, how does that sound?" Gareth asked, as if he was a film director seeking his principal actor.

"Um, hi sorry to interrupt I'm Sara, I was wondering if you heard anything from Ryan or Becky? I texted them today but nothing back, it's kinda weird not to hear from them. Sorry again, just thought you might know something," Sara said sheepishly.

"What?" Gareth spat, as if snapped out of a trance. He heard the words she said but didn't ascribe any meaning to them, it was just noise, noise that disturbed him and broke his reality. Here he was—a teacher and an artist, he was living his fantasy. And now, even in his absence, that filth Ryan was still annoying him with his spawns that he might call friends worrying about his well-being, oh and Becky…Well he quite missed Becky, he dreaded having to form a 'relationship' with one of these cretins, if only he didn't have to kill her, oh but in the moment he had to make a point and that seemed so very necessary.

How else would he have gotten through to that foolish boy Ryan?

Still he would have liked to hear her suggestions, he thought that now he might be able to find another writer to help him but he wanted them to know it was a true story, not based on a true story or fabricated entirely. He wanted them to know that what they were reading and editing was a real thing that happened to real people, although Gareth knew that it couldn't be entirely true. Unfortunately the written word was only a mere replication of the literal truth, there is no such thing as the truth. It is something of the past, intangible, it can be recorded through many means although it is akin to time, a figment and creation of the human imagination. Simply devised to remedy our lack of understanding of a universe beyond our current capabilities. Truths are things that have happened in a certain way that have impacts on our reality. Although if there is no impact, there is no real way to know if something really happened and how. Gareth felt sorrow at his inability to record the true emotions of his victims, he could only ever witness them and never truly understand them. He knew that they had so much to tell, so much to express, all trapped within an obsolete device of a body. If human bodies were truly devices they would have been chucked out and replaced with a more efficient version, although Gareth knew that was the plight of humanity, being trapped within one vessel with limited abilities, destined to die. He was doing them a favor by releasing them from this annoyance which they called life. Gareth knew that life was not a gift, it was a burden shared by all. The way Gareth saw life was like a lake. To him it was as if you were dropped into a lake with many others, all who knew not how to swim, eventually some would learn, some would drown, some would cling onto others to reach the surface, drowning only those under them along with themselves. They could tread water as long as they'd like, some longer than others, eventually everybody goes under.

He knew this was what life was.

Meaningless, a futile meaningless effort.

"Sir? They're a part of the group. You know Becky and Ryan?" Sara repeated, tracing Gareth's inattention.

"Ah, no idea. Although I would like to stress I do not appreciate it when you skip sessions, it is unprofessional and extremely disrespectful. I am profoundly disappointed with Becky and Ryan, to be quite honest I had no faith in either of them. I knew that they would abandon their craft. I have extensive experience with writers, I know what they are like.

You should not miss them. Can we carry on?" Gareth asked hurriedly.

"Um, yeah I guess...Sorry, yeah continue, we can worry about it later. You're probably right," Sara said.

"So where was I?" Gareth said; he had heard Phillip say this and he used it as a refresher.

Gareth knew what talking point he had left off with although he wanted to make it seem as if his students had invited him to return to the subject.

"Something about your life story?" Ben said, who was one of the new students.

"Ah yes, you are right. I wanted to recruit one of the brightest writers from the circle to assist me in the completion of this work, although I would like to remind you it is a highly secretive work and requires the utmost secrecy. I can conduct interviews today and will only be able to see a select number of you. From there we can discuss the matter further, get into your regular writing groups I suppose you have and meanwhile I will take on some of these fine writers," Gareth said.

Reluctantly writers began to find partners to work with for the hour and Gareth scoped out those who were left. Gareth saw Sara who had questioned him on the whereabouts of the missing writers, she would do, usually she partnered up with Ben but today Gareth would request her first.

The two made their way to a set of tables away from the group, Gareth wanted a high level of secrecy for this meeting. He wouldn't tell her anything at the library of course but he wanted to see if she might work. Gareth needed somebody with the know-how to make his life story intriguing, maybe he wouldn't be the traditional hero, he knew that but still wanted to be their anti-hero.

He wanted somebody who could make that happen.

Gareth went through his interview and asked her questions pertaining to his image and how he would be perceived. Sara assured him that if they were working on a biopic that she wouldn't make any hasty changes that he was uncomfortable with. Gareth seemed pleased with the line of questioning and seemed as if he was about done.

Ben was put off by these interviews, he didn't disapprove of this new teacher but there was something about his cadence that made him extremely uncomfortable. Ben knew that sometimes first impressions aren't to be trusted but he felt this through his second, third, and fourth impression, that everything this person did was strange. Gareth seemed as if he was trying to convince Sara into leaving with him somewhere else where they could discuss in private the details of 'his biopic'. Whatever that was he wasn't sure but something sounded off about it. Ben had always asked Phillip if he was working on anything out of the ordinary as Phillip usually had been good with getting Ben work as a freelance writer, they were quite close actually. Usually Phillip met with Ben and Chuck to go over plot details in the novels he was working on, so much as they know he had written three novels in his time, one a fantasy drawing heavily from *Lord of the Rings*, *Harry Potter* and *Beowulf*. He absolutely hated it and never returned to edit the manuscript upon completion. His next stab at writing was a space thriller about a pathogen which could survive in the vacuum of space, one that infests a space station. When he tried to sell it to the publishers—they flushed him off, told him it was far too short and no avid reader would ever find themselves with a copy. Then there was his western novel, this one Ben actually quite liked, although Phillip never finished it and his ending trailed off into a cliff-hanger.

There were two gunmen and they were locked into an impasse over a dispute caused by one of the men being an outlaw by nature, the other was a sheriff and eventually the two stepped on each other's toes in one way or another—they strapped on their iron and then…

Phillip lit a cigar, poured a glass of bourbon and drank away his failures. He was never one for finishing what he started, he would get half-way done and then begin the other half of something he also would never finish. If this Gareth character was telling the truth about the two of them working on a book together then it wouldn't be beyond Ben's imagination. Still, he felt uneasy as if something beyond his understanding was raising a flag about this person in particular, like a sheep suddenly aware of a wolf in the pen. Although the sheep keeps on grazing despite this knowledge, that's its nature.

The bottom line was Gareth was just plain weird, something had to be up, he wondered when Phillip would return, he was much more normal, not acting all strange like this fellow. Ben wouldn't mind a world where more people acted like Phillip if he was being straight with himself. It was about this time when Sara and Gareth rose from their discussion and she began to follow him out of the library without saying goodbye to anyone or Gareth ending the session. Ben wanted to say something but figured Sara would make no objection to going with Gareth in front of him, she was far too polite for that type of behavior. Ben was quite the moralist, but in this moment he decided it might be best to follow them and see where they were headed, just to be safe.

Gareth pushed open the exit to the library and almost collided with the man entering, for he wasn't watching his way out. Phillip wide eyed with his nose running slammed into Gareth, who was holding a stack of books and his laptop.

"Oh my lord!" Phillip exclaimed.

"I—uh was not expecting you back so soon. Let me help you with that there Phillip," Gareth said, trying to piece together the picture that was unraveling before them.

"Leave it, I assure you I am quite capable now." Philip said while gathering the last of his books.

"I do apologize for having you lose your bearings." Gareth said straightening his tie he had tucked into his vest, Phillip looked down at his own tie, also tucked into his vest and started to understand what was happening here.

"Gareth, could you follow me outside for a brief moment?"

"Well we were just off somewhere perhaps it could wait until later?"

"No it cannot, it is of dire attention and that is why I came here to find you, now please will you come?" Phillip said, his eyes displayed a rage that only the person looking into them could truly understand.

Gareth was soon following Phillip through the doors, and without uttering a word—he was quietly ushered outside.

"What in god's name do you think you're doing here?" Phillip shouted.

"I am helping the group in your absence," Gareth said calmly.

"How could you even know I was gone, what kind of decisions have you constructed here Gareth, what exactly is going on? I demand to know!" Phillip demanded.

"Do calm yourself, I may be a killer but I do not like being yelled at."

"Do not say that around here, my you are truly crazy!" Phillip spat.

"I am not crazy Phillip. Do not call me crazy ever again. I came here to replace you. I did enter your study without your permission, I am aware of the fact that you leave your window open and through the stairway access I let myself in. Inside I found no trace of you and it seemed you had been vacant for days by the looks of things. I figured if you were still out and about I might find you at the library with your group as you always discuss with me, I found the address in your study with the collection of names you had shared with me many times. From there I came here and decided I could replace you as it seemed you had not notified these good people of your absence. Therefore, I decided to take up the role of host in your stead. I do not expect you to be angry nor pleased with my service, it was simply out of necessity. I was discussing the book with her to get her opinion; she would have never told anyone but perhaps I should have waited upon your return. You understand."

"You are right in your intentions although I do wish you hadn't done this at all, very well, nothing can be done about it, for the moment at least. I will conclude this session—you are not going anywhere with Sara. I will inquire with you about the whereabouts of Ryan and Becky later, I did not see them inside. Although I fear I need not ask because I already know what their condition must be. Do not do this thing ever again, meet me at my study later-to-nite around six," Phillip told him, then returned inside without saying another thing to him.

Gareth made his way to his old beat up muscle car and ripped that costume he'd put on off of his wiry body, stuffing it into his trunk before slamming it shut with contempt.

He drove off with his usual careless speed.

Sara and Ben witnessed this scene from inside and were severely taken aback.

"What was all that if you don't mind my asking?" Sara asked Phillip.

"We had creative differences on the biopic he discussed with you, the fellow tore off in a fit, he'll get over it, I assure you."

"You picked this guy yourself?" Ben asked, perplexed.

"Sometimes we aren't left with many options when we're on the chopping block my dear boy, now let's all gather round so we can discuss all your progress that I might have missed."

11

"Campylobacter, it is a very common foodborne illness. I induced the creation of it in some contaminated water that I collected. I then exchanged this for the water used in Phillip's tea. For the usual person you might run into the habit of them having to boil the water, effectively killing any disease you might have bidden upon them. But you see Phillip has this awful habit of microwaving his tea, he happens to be the type to make it and never drink it, too consumed in his work, then too lazy to make another cup. So, I simply switched out the tea hoping for my plan to work. It did. When I found him absent the next couple days, I waited for his classes to begin. And...well that is when I met you and my life changed for the better. That is my form of a joke, my life changed not for the better but as your life might change when you purchase a pet and realize you no longer want to care for it and long for the day of its death. That is how I feel about you," Gareth told Ryan.

"Why are you always telling me things, I'm not your therapist—can you fuck off?" Ryan choked out.

"I am telling you things because I need someone who will not tell a soul what I am saying. I tell you these things not for your insight or your advice but as a means of airing out my ideas so that they become more clear to me, it has nothing to do with you personally in any way. You are simply a warm body that will interpret what I am saying and I will make no use of the chatter you produce. You are right though, I will 'fuck off' eventually. After I have buried you in your own backyard of course, and after I redecorate your interior because, oh how awful your choice is. Everything is covered in blood; you need a new decorator," Gareth said, feigning a coy smile.

"Shut up, please. I'm done with all of it. If you'd just kill me maybe I'd respect you a sliver, it's strange, you've been torturing me so long I'm past terrified. I'm actually annoyed, and you can't be annoyed and terrified at the same time, you always put me on drugs to talk to me and when you let them fade I'm in pain but I pass out after a bit. There's nothing else you can do, except for shutting the fuck up, taking that knife dragging it across my neck and being done with it," Ryan said plainly.

"You do not make the decisions, you are my possession now, you are my pet. I will dispose of you when you have served your purpose, then you will be buried out back like the animal you are. Never have I felt dislike for someone until I met you, I think you should know this."

"Oh, out of what? The fifteen people you've met in your life? Or all the ones you met on your nights out kidnapping and murdering old people with an axe? I'm sure it's a great way to meet people nowadays," Ryan somehow found himself joking.

"You are not funny, stop trying to remedy your suffering with humor. I am not amused by your antics. Keep it up and I will slice your hands clean off you imbecile."

"Oh no, I'll miss them dearly, it's not as if someone…already took off all my fingers or something," Ryan said, dozing off due to the painkillers.

"I will not let you take advantage of my emotions; your hands stay on, I have other plans and I will follow them because it is for my art and you will not ruin the art I make of you."

"God damn, I have no fingers and I've been on and off tortured—but the last feeling I would expect is being tired, fucking crazy, absolutely mad." Ryan started to hysterically laugh.

"This is not funny and you are not allowed to laugh."

"It's too late, I don't care anymore, you have nothing to threaten me with," Ryan chuckled.

Gareth on the other hand grew red in the cheeks with rage, he picked up a heavy vase off one of the counters and shattered it over Ryan's head, knocking him unconscious. Huffing out his breath Gareth charged out of the house, slamming the door so hard it rumbled within its frame.

12

It was just about six in the afternoon. Phillip had been writing in his study for hours now, calmly puffing on his pipe when suddenly someone started wrapping on his door as if they were throwing themselves against the frame.

"I'll be there in a second! Hold your horses!" Phillip shouted over the knocking, opening the door and much to his surprise he set eyes on a clearly perturbed Gareth.

He was huddled in upon himself and extremely reserved, something was amiss.

"Why, Gareth! What seems to be the problem?" Phillip asked with feign concern.

Gareth pushed past him like a pedestrian on a subway.

"You seem to be the problem, you are stalling, you are lazy and you have not finished my book, if you have you won't show it to me and I've had enough of you," Gareth said in a huff, as he did Phillip handed him a hefty stack of papers, titled 'Manuscript #1'.

"There you are my boy, it pains me how long it did take—although I feel that you will find it worth the wait, it is truly a marvelous work of mine I must say," Philip said while patting Gareth on the back.

"That is all I have asked of you Phillip, I apologize for my outburst. It seems you have made good on your promise," Gareth said, flipping through the pages.

"So I expect you will read it and get back to me as soon as you can?" Phillip asked.

"Yes, I'll call for you when I'm finished," Gareth said plainly, taking a seat in Phillip's luxurious leather-bound chair.

"You're staying?" Phillip asked, quite perturbed.

"Phillip, please, don't break my concentration." Gareth hushed him with a wave of the hand.

Without pause Gareth began reading, and to his surprise, it was an absolute masterpiece. Truly for once in his life, he felt happy. Never before had he been familiar with the feeling of happiness. Gareth smiled, he never really thought about smiling, if he had ever done this before out of joy—he did not remember.

When he completed his reading, Gareth's smile faded, it had been an amazing book. One which did him great justice and he looked spectacular. Yet none of this brought him any asylum from his pain, the pain he felt each day which he escaped from through his art, it all felt as if it was leading up to this big thing and once this thing happened everything might be okay. Nothing felt better, it felt exactly the same.

Gareth figured he must not be thinking straight, of course this was important. He had to remember that it wasn't the book that would make him revered as an artist, it was the reception of the book that mattered. What a fool he was, obviously there was no satisfaction to completing a project if you were unable to share it with anyone. What good is a miracle witnessed by one man? There is no reason to show off in the company of one. He decided he would await the publication of his book and suspend his excitement until then, for now he placed the manuscript on the end table in Phillip's study and would wait for the next big thing to happen. Gareth scooped up his phone and called Phillip at home to announce his completion, it was four thirty seven in the morning at this time.

The Killing Stroke

Phillip Fairview

Phillip Fairview's Introduction

What is art? Some may say a painting is a work of art, another may regard an obscure collection of junk as art and even yet all are equally as valid. What do we mean when we say something is art? Is it thought provoking? For many things are thought provoking, an Antelope being eaten by a lion is thought provoking, does this make that art? If a man is killed on the news and you hear of it, this may provoke thought, does that make their murder art? Is the act of killing in fact a long forgotten art or, a long-dismissed one, for fear of the true nature of our being? If you think of our entertainment all we watch are films involving blood and gore and murder, now if you see a film with these elements you enjoy you might regard it as good. Now remember films are seen as a work of art by many, yet with the elements of murder in an action movie you would by association be classifying murder as an art, although a facade of such an act, why do we adore it so? Do we desire murder but resent the pain it causes, is this what spews our interest in the fake murder on television, or is it something more? Do we not only watch action movies, or perhaps do we also watch 'true' crime films. Based on a true story that has brought in many from their homes to witness a true event, something of this validity gives rise to a higher peak of interest than your regular run of the mill chainsaw wielding maniac might. When he is a real chainsaw wielding maniac we hurry to the popcorn stand and take our seats, why? You must enjoy it on some level, murder must be an art on some level. In fact I would argue it is an art, on every level. For I will reveal to you a friend of mine, his name is Gareth and he is what you would classify as a murderer, yet I regard him as my good friend. He is an artist and I have looked upon many of his works in wonder, his

102

works have been at times inspired by myself and others he has taken to his own guidance and taken the creative license to produce amazing slaughter in his time. We never thought when beginning this project that it might become such a cornerstone of artistic display until we had finished our collaboration. It has truly taken on a life of its own, this story is about a struggling artist in a medium unrecognized and even prosecuted. His bravery and willingness to overcome all odds will make this a classic for years to come, Gareth hopes one day you will read this in your english class and study it as you might Hamlet or Macbeth, it is truly deserving of such a mantle. I have these hopes as well, yet on your first reading I do hope you enjoy my detailed descriptions of these imaginative works of art.

-Phillip Faiview

14

Zipping up his tracksuit he began to pace as he adjusted his headphones and turned on a song, music began to play into Gareth's ears and he began his moonlight jog. Tucking his garrotte wire into his pocket, Gareth set off at a medium pace while jiggling his shoulders to the beat, the air felt entirely refreshing tonight.

As he approached a man wearing an orange tracksuit—he quickly met his pace and wrapped the wire around his neck, strangling him while jiving to the music. Gareth pressed his elbow up against the man's back while surveying in the distance to ensure nobody could see them, turning purple the man swatted back at Gareth with his hands trying to get him off. When he heard the crack Gareth released the wire, the body fell flat on its face with a splitting thud, he tucked his wire back into his pocket and began to lift the heavy limp body into the bushes.

Another runner was seen in the distance, she came running by and he almost hadn't noticed her as she jotted by. With lightning speed he snagged her and pulled her into the bushes. Within a few seconds he heard his snap and pushed off her, then he heard another snap.

Something else had moved in the bushes, Gareth's heart jumped from his chest. As he straightened himself and moved from the bushes—he saw a rabbit burst out after him.

What a spook that had been!

Without another thought Gareth continued his jog, he reached a bridge and began to shuffle his feet in tandem and carried a smooth rhythm as he did.

He saw a man dressed in all white running towards him, underneath the bridge. Gareth waited until he got closer and then procured his hefty cinder block, similar to one playing an arcade game he waited until the time was just right to let the concrete slip between his fingers, and with momentous impact— utterly devastated the skull of the man below. The man's white tracksuit transmogrified into a dark red surrounded in a bloody slush, chunks of bone were scattered among the runner's path. He'd leave that for someone else to clean up, Gareth felt he had done enough work for today. Perhaps he'd write about it later, he couldn't wait until the day his book was published and then he could do this sort of thing more often. He'd like that.

15

When the cops arrived on the scene, they came upon a

plethora of human bodies lying around the park,

disposed of with ease in plain sight as one would with

littered trash. They were aghast and disturbed at the

crime scene, one of the chief officers stepped through

the bloody pile of bones and blood carefully to

approach the scene.

"Excuse me ma'am, you placed the call?"

Officer Brody asked.

"That was me," Shelley replied.

"Hi, I'm police chief Brody, but feel free to

call me Amelia if you like. I've got my officers

looking around, we'll draw up a crime scene, I can take

your statement if you'd like," Officer Brody said.

"Ok," Shelley said, walking over while putting

out her fifth cigarette in the fifteen minutes that passed

since she placed her panicked call. "I was running and I just saw a bunch of dead people. It's just fucked up, I don't understand who would do this sort of thing it's just—" She began to tear up.

"That's all I need, thank you," Brody said, easing off.

"Christ! There's another body in the bushes!" An officer shouted from a distance.

"All right, I want a search party out now, close the park at all entrances and the surrounding area I want blocked off until we secure the area!" Officer Brody barked to the surrounding officers.

Officer Brody then walked over to the man with the cinderblock in his head, it wasn't a pretty sight. There weren't any fingerprints on the block, blood was splattered everywhere along the path like a sickening version of an abstract.

The strangled woman and man were hidden in the same bush using wire, that was obvious, but Brody noticed a strand of hair clinging to the fingers of the man. It was noticeably darker than his own hair and so it was collected as evidence, so the killer had dark brown hair.

'Interesting' thought Brody, it wasn't much but it was something.

"Excuse me ma'am I'm sorry to bother you, but did you see anyone with dark brown hair wandering the park, perhaps on their own?"

"There was one guy, I think he must have gone down the path over to Riverson Street."

"Alright you heard her, get some squad cars over to Riverson! And ma'am if you should require any psychological counseling, we have the resources available to you, just let me know if that's something we can offer. Otherwise, I can also offer transportation to wherever you might live, I'm assuming you jogged here and are not insistent on jogging back."

"Would you be?"

"No. You want that ride?" Officer Brody asked, Shelley lethargically raised a hand and followed Brody to the cruiser.

Slapping the door shut, Shelley got in the passenger seat, the engine whirled to a start and they departed from that god-awful park.

"So where is it you live?"

"Just up the street here, I know it's not far but as we've covered, there's sort of a maniac running around here, god makes my skin crawl to think about him just lurking about. You will find him won't you?" Shelley asked.

"That's the thing with killers, they have a way of revealing themselves. This was messy, no doubt he'll slip up a bit more the next time and eventually he'll give himself away. I guarantee he'll tell a couple of his buddies and they'll tell two friends and they'll come shaking through our phone lines with an anonymous tip, just follow the paper trail."

"So you think he'll kill again?"

"Just make sure you lock your doors for the next couple days."

16

"Oh this is bad, this is very…Bad." Phillip said, flicking off the television in his study. Gareth was sitting on his sofa while he began to understand fully what he had done. Gareth came to Phillip as soon as he saw the buzz around his killings, he was ecstatic and ran to tell Phillip that it was his best work yet and insisted it be added to the novel.

"Oh, you silly boy! You must never speak of this to me again, you've drawn quite an audience and the book hasn't even touched shelves yet! You just can't help yourself, it's quite ridiculous. Why I've never seen anyone quite like yourself, if you asked me I'd say your worst character trait is that incessant need for attention you have. You put us in quite hot water this time," Phillip ranted.

"I would like to remind you that you are best to watch the tone in which you regard me, if I claim that I want my art added to the novel, then it will be added per my request. Do not challenge me on this, it is to be written in the style I devise and with the content I decide."

"Why yes of course, that was never a question, although I would need to alter some areas of the text I believe I meet your demands, is this suitable?"

"That would be suitable."

"Well then it's settled, I'll have the edited copy to you by tomorrow my dear boy; I'll have you know that we're due to hit shelves in a week, so this will be hard to pull off."

"Oh I think they are going to love it; I had the reader in mind during those artistic splurges at the park. I knew they would adore such a scene. They always do."

17

Phillip was now enjoying his book signings and press junkets. Gareth, on the other hand, was not as pleased with this book. He had gone to purchase one for himself in secret, Phillip promised to get him a copy but Gareth simply could not help himself. Strolling through the aisles Gareth found himself eyeing those who picked up the novel, it took every fiber in his body to restrain himself from informing him he was the artist in the book; he figured it wasn't the place anyhow and enjoyed the anonymity. He overheard a conversation concerning the book while in the checkout line.

"Oh this one is marvelous, my husband picked it up for me the other night and I just couldn't get enough of it. It was just sickening; I mean usually I can't stand stuff like that but the story was so good that I couldn't put it down!" The cashier said.

"Don't spoil it! I'm looking forward to reading it, I might skip some parts if they get too graphic though, I know—I'm bad!" The girl buying the book said as she giggled, paid and left with a wave to the cashier, along with a shouted thanks.

Gareth was not impressed with their impression of the book, people were not seeing it as artistic. They even said they might skip the entire sections where he describes his art! Could you imagine such a world where that was acceptable? The absolute horror. This was incredibly annoying; Gareth made his way to the cashier and slammed the book onto the table.

"You know I was just telling the last customer about this book, that Garth guy is a real nasty fellow! You'll find out soon enough, I don't want to spoil it for you but that guy is a complete sicko!"

"You think this book is good?" Gareth asked.

"Everyone says so."

"Because everyone says so, that makes it good?"

"Well no, but generally people are right about these types of things and I think I understand what the author was going for."

"I do not think you understand the author one bit! In fact your appraisal of the book leads me to believe you read things without a single care or thought in your mind. You most likely read it once while watching a television program and therefore failed to pick up on important plot points. I am actually a friend of the author and closely related the events that transpired in the story. It is based on a true story and I know those events better than anyone who's read that book yet! I was very instrumental in the writing of this book and you have completely misread what it was about! Good day, I am taking this book, it practically belongs to me in any case!" Gareth shouted at the poor woman; he blew through the sliding doors and peeled out of the parking lot in a hurry—then accidentally slammed into another parked car, shredding the front bumper off and leaving it lying on the asphalt.

Gareth flew down the road in his car, heading straight for Phillip's book signing; he'd been having them at libraries ever since the release. Gareth called him on the phone several times, no response, he'd even broken into his study to find everything neatly packaged in boxes—which Gareth took extra care to tear apart and damage.

Gareth was fuming, Phillip had been dodging him ever since the release date. Gareth found out that day at the bookstore that the book had in fact embellished most of the key points of the story. Why the hell was it stated that all events were embellished or fictionalized and if anything relates to the real world it should be written off as coincidence? Gareth had not

117

read anything like this in his early copy of the book, it was completely as he liked it. This was not his book in the backseat, it was some hack of an author riding his coattails is what it was, he was about to give Phillip a piece of his mind and demand republication!

Phillip saw a bright light shine in through the doors of the library, it looked to be Gareth's vehicle. He timidly scraped his pen across the next book placed in front of him and slid it to his left, he unconsciously shook someone's hand and bid them farewell, his eyes remained trained on the door. Bursting through was Gareth, practically foaming at the mouth, holding his copy of the novel between his greasy fingers. He slammed the book down onto the table.

"Who should I make it out to?" Phillip asked, grabbing the book.

"I only brought the book to get through the line Phillip, you know who I am, I'm Gareth! Or have you forgotten? Oh that's right, you forgot most of what

118

I specifically requested, you are making a mockery of my work! This is all my doing, you know I was the one behind everything, yet you lie to these people and tell them it's fake! Merely a picture contrived in your thick skull, if it was up to me I'd smash it in with a mallet you no good hack!"

"Please calm down sir, there's no need for this, I haven't the slightest idea what you're talking about. Why, everyone knows this book is made up, it always has been. I made it up myself in my study. It's truly outrageous the lengths you people will go to claim fame from those who've worked tirelessly to produce art!"

"Art! You call this art, it's no good shit, our original copy was art. This is a hack job for the masses! I was the only artist ever involved in this story, when you sent me to kill those people I brought back amazing notes to review and every good murder in this book was calculated and executed by me! Not you, you old fool, nothing you've ever done was artistic, all you do is sit in your study and smoke cigars you fat slog, shame on you! You're reading a bastardized text, you're all bastards for it! Pretend you don't know me, fine, that's all good and well, I'll publish my own version and these people will learn the truth about what happened! What do you think I am, what do you think I do?" Gareth boasted arrogantly—as he saw Phillip's fans as mindless sheep, behaving just as he expected. They were all lining up to get their beloved murder story scrawled on.

"Security, could you please remove this man. He is unwell," Phillip stated.

"You can't hide behind a flimsy table forever Phillip! I'm coming for you! I'm coming for you!" Gareth screamed at him. Eventually the crowd began clapping as Gareth was forcefully removed, and soon enough another fan brought their book up to be signed.

"That was quite a show, how'd you think of that?" The fan asked.

"What do you mean?" Phillip asked.

"You hired someone to play Gareth, absolutely amazing! I know you can't say though cause then it'd be ruined. It was very cool, everyone seemed to like it," The fan said before thanking him for the signature.

After the signing had concluded there were many articles written surrounding the incident, all positive and congratulating Phillip on bringing an immersive and fun aspect to his book signing. It seemed he'd gotten away with it after all, Phillip read them all on his phone, and when he was pleased he powered it off and placed it into the cupholder in his new car, a beautiful red sports thing. He'd slid in a CD and skipped to his favorite Frank Sinatra song, "Killing Me Softly". As the melody led into the lyrical flow he slightly edged his foot on the gas pedal and took himself away from the book singing. Phillip felt magical; he felt like his car was floating across the road, taking him to his gloriously large mansion. Upon arrival, his magnificent gates opened to receive him. The drive towards his home from this point on would provide ample time to enjoy the meticulous nature of the masterpiece. Phillip savored the ending of the song then ripped his keys from the vehicle and slammed the vehicle door shut as he shimmied to his doorstep, practically clicking his heels. Everything he ever wanted was in front of him, he was a respected author, he had an enormous home, an enormous fan base and the critics loved him! Could you imagine!

   Gareth though, that was tricky he thought as he splashed his keys into his key-dish. What to do about that foolish boy? Why couldn't he just be happy with what he was given, he did more than enough for that creature. He didn't even deserve the respect he gave him, he wasn't even going to use his first name but did anyway! How ungrateful Gareth was acting. Of course he had to fictionalize his surname, but it had a better flow anyhow. Gareth Michevich. Nice. That's why he gets paid the big bucks he thought. For coming up with such clever names like that.

He was a writer, finally.

Then he had it! Phillip had a wonderfully awful idea. He would make an anonymous call to the police about Gareth and where they could find him. He would do this from a pay phone of course, otherwise they may begin to suspect him. Phillip wondered if they might already suspect him as is, he did write that everything was fictional and not based on reality or whatever, but what if the police were able to read in between the lines and figure out that it was all true after all.

No.

Better not to think like that.

It would just serve to stress the old goel out unnecessarily. He was already stressed enough over that whole episode with Gareth. The boy had no right to barge in there making demands of him, he thought.

By what right?

He didn't write the damn thing!

It was Phillip, him and only him who wrote the book. Gareth didn't deserve any of that money. He was a disgusting murderer, as Phillip knew. He told himself that he was righteous for not engaging in any of the murders, he simply gave the boy a push out the door. Really Phillip felt like more of a narrator of the boy's sick and twisted delights. He had nothing to do with it, is what he would tell himself before he fell asleep each night.

Now he would make the call and they'd never be the wiser. 'Goodbye Gareth!' Phillip thought; it wasn't a pleasure.

18

Slowly approaching the target, he went for the wrists and wrestled the man to the ground, he struggled against his restraints, but it was no use. There'd be no struggling at all in a moment; he dragged him across the sidewalk and onto the road.

It was all over in an instant; Gareth had been thrown into the back of a police cruiser.

As it turns out; that anonymous call they received had been accurate after-all. Brody doubted they'd find the guy—let alone catch him, it was a good day for the force, and the community.

They'd arrested him as he was leaving.

In his pockets they found a boning knife, a screwdriver and a pair of wired headphones.

"I've been set-up! This is preposterous, a man isn't allowed to go on a peaceful jog anymore without being harassed by the police?" Gareth raved as they had got him.

"And who set you up?" Brody asked.

"It was *him*! Phillip Fairview."

"Who?"

"Phillip Fairview, he is a writer. He is trying to pin everything on me!"

"And what's everything?"

"Oh, you are clever! Everything is whatever you think I have done."

"It's what we know you've done. There's enough evidence already to put you away for good."

"You lock away what you fear, but I am not to fear. I am just an artist."

"Uh huh."

"You will see. I am going to finish my book and then you will see."

"What book?"

"It is going to be called *The Killing Stroke: The Real Truth*,"

"As in the book that's already out? Why don't you write your own thing?"

"It is my own thing! Phillip is a thief, and a criminal. You should be arresting him, not me!"

"So you're saying you didn't do it?"

"I am not a criminal."

Brody produced the boning knife, "Well then would you care to explain why we found this in your pocket?" One of Brody's eyebrows raised. "Nothing to say?"

"Oh. On the contrary, I have much to say….although I doubt you'd be able to stomach it."

"I'm sure. I've been on the force for six years, seen worse than you. By the way, I'd like to remind you that everything you say can and will be used against you in the court of law. Hope you're able to stomach that."

"You threaten *me*? Do you know who I am? Do you know what I'm capable of? I should gut you where you stand, you filthy whore!"

"That's all I need." Brody slammed the cruiser door shut on Gareth while he shouted, unfortunately nobody could hear him scream.

19

He wasn't sure about this. But then again, he wasn't
quite sure of anything after what he'd gone through.
When he'd finally been taken care of, the doctors told
him the pain meds alone should have killed him. Not to
mention the physical and emotional trauma he suffered
at the hands of that maniac. Nonetheless, it did get him
a solid book deal. Go figure, before the incident
nobody would lay a hand on his work. Now they were
having bidding wars on who was going to get to sell
his story; one of the bigger few got a hold of it, that's
where the money was.

Anyhow, he'd hired his own typist to write up
the thing for him while he described how it should all
sound. Him not being able to type didn't restrict him
one bit, in fact he actually preferred this method to
traditional writing, say your ideas out loud and

magically have them transcribed onto paper. He only

wished that it had been that easy from the start. Things

might have turned out a lot easier, gone a lot different.

Was it so bad though? Considering all the possibilities,

the way things could have gone. Was he lucky? He

didn't feel lucky. Getting away from something like

that, something so scarring, you'd think you'd feel

relief at least. Maybe there'd be more long-lasting

relief had he never survived, only he knew that was

just the self-pity talking. In reality he was lucky to

escape death, or was that his fear of death talking? He

used to think he knew everything. Now he knows that

he knows nothing. When your whole concept of reality

is shattered, you start to look around and wonder, does

anybody know what the fuck they're doing? The

answer is usually no, if they do then they know what

they're doing is pointless and do it anyway. Maybe

they're stupid, or maybe they're smart, or maybe they

know it doesn't matter what they are. Whatever anything was, he didn't care much anymore.

The strangest gift he was given from the trauma was an incredible amount of apathy. He'd finally gotten what he wanted. This was *his* book signing, he'd done it, he'd made it. Why did he feel so empty? Incomplete? He was told all his fans were waiting outside, they'd been there for hours while he was getting prepared. Well that's not entirely true, he'd been ready to sign for hours. His staff was getting prepared. For what he had no clue, he was the one signing the damn books. It would be tricky however; he didn't know how well he would fare with his prosthetics, but if not then his typist could always sign. She did write the thing after all, inside he always felt it was more her book than his. His book was sitting on the shelf back at home, finished and never to be read. It was the one he finished with Becky, dreams of getting it published died with her. Now he was a commodity for his life story and not for the story he'd been writing all his life. In the outside world he was told that the only thing important about him was what happened to him, a terrible thing. He wouldn't ever be given the luxury of forgetting the whole thing, not that he ever could if he tried. Unfortunately, the public only cares about *that* story. So that was the story he would have to sell, unless he wanted to become mentally scarred *and* homeless.

"Are you ready?"

Suddenly, he found he wasn't. He couldn't answer, his breath hid deep inside his lungs. Ryan nodded yes, he was ready.

They flooded through the doors like water, clamoring to get their spot in line. Ryan never understood the rush, by anyone, ever. Where could you possibly need to get that you disregard others to get there? Sure, people might convince themselves that where *they* need to get is more important than others.

It's not. Nothing other than life and death is so important that you should need to rush to get there. Maybe you might be able to get something done five minutes quicker, but now it's five minutes worse for the wear. Funnily enough, Ryan saw calm people assume the spots in line directly behind those who were rushing. The only thing you get for rushing is people thinking you're an idiot, that and getting nowhere fast.

Ryan always thought that he wanted a book deal, that he wanted the attention. He didn't want any of that. Obviously he wanted people to read his work but he enjoyed workshopping his ideas. Working with Becky and imagining people's responses to his work. They'd love this character; they'd hate this one. You always sort of knew how your audience would respond to a certain type of character, although sometimes they would surprise you.

Here was the first fan, she'd pushed her way to the front of the line and was out of breath and gasping. She gripped the book in her sweaty hands like it was her newborn child, which would have concerned him considering how hard she slammed it onto the table in front of him. She did so as if she was giving him a stack of papers he had to have on her desk by noon, it was done with such an attitude as to say 'hurry up, I've been waiting'. Even though by the looks of it, the people behind her had been the ones waiting. Ryan looked up to his publicist and queued their reaction to give him a pen, it wasn't like he could up and grab one for himself. His prosthetic shook due to the essential tremor he had developed, he quivered and he wondered how he was going to sign all of the copies coming his way.

"Who should I make it out to?"

"Could you make it out to Gareth?"

Ryan held the quivering pen in his hand and his shaking intensified until the pen dropped out of his hand. Without question the publicist simply replaced the pen in his hand and retreated. Ryan returned a blank stare to the fan.

"I'm Liv. I was thinking I could give it to him, I plan on paying him a visit when they allow visitations. I'm actually his type, he'd probably murder me, don't you think?"

Ryan continued staring blankly ahead.

"So, are you going to sign it?"

"Don't think—" Ryan began as he was cut off by his publicist grabbing his shoulder.

"We haven't got much time, just sign the damn thing!" She shouted to him, as if he was the one being unreasonable.

Fine, he'd sign it.

Inside, he wrote as best he could 'To my best friend Gareth, I hope you enjoy it!'.

You ask a dumbass question; you get a smartass response.

"Thanks." The fan said, rolling her eyes, as if he pissed *her* off.

People these days, then came another. Then came a question about Gareth.

 "Where's Gareth these days?"

"Oh he's in Florida, we're keeping in touch, pen pals actually."

"That's awesome, I'm surprised you forgave him, good for you."

'Are you fucking stupid?' Ryan thought.

In what world did she live where a murderer was just hanging out in Florida getting letters from one of his victims. Probably the same one Gareth did. He let it go, there were countless others waiting in line. Here came another, she seemed more normal than the last, she'd actually given up her spot for the guy ahead of her. The last guy didn't say much though, just asked for the signature. He was probably going to sell it and said something about getting the whole set of signatures. Ryan hoped he didn't mean what he thought he meant. Anyway, this next woman's smile was glowing with friendly energy and she handed him the book, it fell from his grasp but she still made the effort to hand it to him. Her boyfriend tried to pick it up for him but Ryan shooed him away and insisted on getting it himself.

"Who should I make it out to?"

"Oh, it's for my younger cousin, she just loves true crime stories. It's kinda our thing."

"It's our thing too!" Her boyfriend chimed in.

"I know but it was our thing way before it was *our* thing."

"What's her name, your cousin?"

"Oh sorry, Rebecca. You can just write Becky though."

It was like she'd shot him in the chest. There goes that pen again, he'd dropped it a second time. Again, the publicist replaced it.

"Oh, I'm so sorry. I forgot that they've got the same name."

"Who?" Her boyfriend asked.

"His friend who was killed by the guy in the book, she has the same name as my cousin."

"Oh, the guy you got the tattoo for?"

"*Yes*, that guy."

What guy? Tattoo? Ryan was confused but said nothing.

"Oh, do you wanna see?"

Did he? Well, he was going to see it anyway he presumed. Before he could respond she was rolling up her sweater sleeve, revealing the names of serial killers covering her arm.

"I was going to get all the killers on one arm and the victims on the other, but there were too many of them, I try to stay on top of it but it's just impossible sometimes."

"I don't get it, do you *like* serial killers?" Ryan asked.

"*No!* I hate them, I just find them interesting. Like, *why would you do that*? Why would anyone do that? I just like getting in their heads and figuring them out. What went wrong, stuff like that."

"So why the tattoos?"

Her boyfriend chimed in, "I know, I told her to get my name if you're just gonna get some weirdo killers on your arm anyway but she said—"

"I just think it's cool to have. And babe, don't talk out of turn. I thought we worked on this."

"Okay," Ryan said, removing himself from the equation.

In the book he wrote 'To Becky, stay safe out there'. He handed it back to the fan with considerable effort and saw Gareth's name flash out at him as she reached out to grab it.

"Anything else I can do?"

She read the inscription and smiled.

"No, that's great! Thanks a lot. You stay safe too."

He hadn't even thought of that, after a traumatic event the world wants you to believe that the past is behind you. What they don't tell you is that the future isn't guaranteed and something much worse could be waiting around the corner. He wasn't immune to violence just because he suffered at the hands of a monster. He was just aware of it now; he didn't know if that was better or worse.

He never imagined his fame and success this way, it wasn't about this book surely.

These weren't his fans; they were Gareth's fans. Maybe they just didn't know it.

20

Faint humming, the sleeping guard woke up from his morning nap to faint humming. This man was extremely bewildered, in all his forty years of working as a prison guard he had never heard a prisoner so much as sing a single musical intonation to himself. Here, without opening his eyelids he might have imagined he was in a fine garden while it was being cheerfully trimmed. No, this was a hole, the walls were gray and cracked, the floors were cold and intrusive. Who the fuck was singing in this piece of shit? Coming into the eyeshot of the prison cell Wade came face to face with this cheerful prisoner, he was just finishing his story, written on the placid wall in blood scrawled text, he was just finishing the letters a-top reading Chapter One. Wade saw the man's cellmate lying face down with his neck opened at the base.

"What do you think? Be honest," Gareth said,

fingers dripping with blood.

21

"How did it make you feel?"

"Good."

"Killing someone makes you feel good?"

"Sometimes."

"Is that why you killed him?"

"No."

"Why did you kill him?"

"Nobody gave me a pen."

"A pen?"

"Writing utensils are required for writing."

"You wanted to write?"

"My story of course. You may have heard of it?"

"What story is this?"

"Ah. So, have you not heard of it?"

"I might have, but just so we're both familiar about what we're discussing enlighten me."

"Well, seeing as you are not up to date with the news," Gareth cleared his throat. "I am highlighted in a famous book which has just recently been showcased in many bookstores across the country. Unfortunately though it is filled with many lies, I am in the process of fixing these errors."

"So this was all over a pen?" The question was asked.

The answer was absent.

For some time the two of them sat in silence while a fly landed onto Gareth's face, it began to crawl up his cheek and over the prominent bones beneath his skin. Closer until it almost reached his eyeball, it rubbed together its arms as if it knew what it was about to do. Crawling across Gareth's bare eyeball, the fly sat unmoved for brief moments that felt like hours.

"Gareth, the question."

144

Blinking his eyes Gareth startled the fly away, it landed on his hand and began to prod its tiny legs around, moving towards the desk.

Gareth trapped it by its wing under his thumb.

"How fast do you think you can make it to the door?" Gareth asked.

"I'm sorry?"

"How fast. Do you think? You could. *Make it to the door*."

"I don't think that I, I don't think…that I follow."

"You follow."

"I um—Gareth, how would you feel about ending a little early today?"

"Early? Oh, but I had much more to share with you. I was beginning to enjoy our little conversation."

"Yes I…I think we could continue next week. We've covered a lot of ground. Next week." The doctor rose from his seat and quickly made his way to the door.

'Too slow' Gareth thought as he crushed the fly under his thumb.

Outside the room, the doctor met with the officers waiting at the door. They all had intrigued looks painted on their faces, anxiously awaiting the doctor's feedback.

"Well, what'd you think?" The police chief asked.

"I recommend he takes antipsychotics as soon as possible. Speak to my office and they will be able to recommend some options."

"Will we be seeing you next week?"

"I will not be returning."

Inside the room Gareth smiled.

22

"You're canceling on me?"

"No I'm not canceling I'm just…"

"You're just what? You're just canceling on me!"

"Ron you know it's not like that…I just can't. I can't do it."

"Well then I can't write you a paycheck."

"That's bullshit! I've already done most of the fucking tour!"

"You didn't sign a contract for *most* of the work, if you read it, like I assumed an author would, you'd know that if you don't make your appearances, the money—held in escrow, is returned."

"You think that's right?"

"Yeah it's fair, this is a company with people who work eight hour shifts to make sure your book

147

lands on shelves. What should we do instead, pay people for not doing work and leave all our employees without paychecks because an author doesn't *feel* like doing promotion? Get real."

Click.

The line went dead and Ryan threw the phone.

Unfortunately he owned a new phone and not a landline, so the thing smashed into tiny pieces and scattered itself across the laminate hardwood floor in his new home. That kind of mess always took a while to clean up, even afterwards you always had a chance of stepping the wrong way when your guard was down to get a nicely opened cut.

Truth be told, he had no idea what he was going to do. Sure the book sales had lined his pocket quite nicely but he'd poured it into his mortgage, which wasn't even fully paid off yet. He also had the car which was actually paid off, but it still cost him a hefty price tag. His royalties were few and far between, the book had an initial burst of interest that quickly died down. So he was left with only one option, he either called Ron back and resumed his tour, or he sold his home, his fancy car and all the other accompaniments.

Not to mention the fact that he would no longer be able to afford his typist, that meant he'd *virtually* never write again. He would always try speech to text but that was a nightmare. The prosthetics helped but not enough. His hand would cramp up, he'd get frustrated and break some things. Then that would be the end of whatever small inspiration he was able to drum up that particular day.

His typist, Diana, helped him with everything, his temperament and his ideas. If he was stuck she'd recommend he go into the theater room (yes he had a theater room, go figure) and review some of the movies that she always saw him light up after watching. It was in these ways that she not only wrote for him, but also gave him the inspiration to write in the first place. If he'd lost her he could surely find a cheaper alternative, but it wouldn't be the same quality without Diana around. It was needless to say but Diana would still help Ryan despite his lack of monetary value to her, she wasn't just offering the extra assistance because he paid her to. Not to mention that he surely didn't pay her extra when she stayed late because she knew he needed more time to workout his ideas. Diana never mentioned how late they'd been working, when Ryan *did* notice he would make a comment about giving her overtime—and would always forget. Not that she cared in the first place.

Ryan would never notice the small things, but he did notice the big picture. He knew his work was better in her presence and he was afraid of losing that valuable influence.

On his work, of course.

Ryan working on his own was a nightmare, he'd planned for his writing to start at six.

Generally he missed this timeslot, and he ended the night by lying in his bed with a lumpy stress blanket while scrolling through agreeable movies on his current favorite streaming service.

"Are you done in there?" Diana asked.

"Yeah, you can come back in," Ryan said. He had a habit of locking himself in his bedroom during important calls.

Inside he would begin to pace and talk, pace and talk.

"I was wondering how long you were gonna take on that goddamn phone, what was the noise? What did you throw?"

"My...Phone..."

"I just picked that up for you after you smashed the last one. Well, I hope you like using the landline because you're gonna go bankrupt at this rate.

Maybe you can live in a house made up of all the glass I've swept off of the floor."

"Yeah well maybe you can stick to typing instead of joking."

"He who lives in a glass house should not throw phones."

"Wow... I can't believe that despite his busy schedule *Eddie Murphy* has the time to make jokes in my house!" That got him a pillow to the head, Diana had plucked it from his bed and launched it playfully at him.

Diana shot back, "Oh and I suppose you're some great comedian yourself now aren't you?"

"Well I mean I don't want to hurt your feelings, but I'm opening for Rodney Dangerfield next week actually."

"Really, has CGI gotten that good? Can they bring him back? Do they *have the technology*?"

"Oh you wouldn't believe it, they're actually going to have Rickles middle so I'm kinda nervous but not that—" She cut him off with a kiss, and Ryan's shocked expression pulled her back.

"What's the matter?"

"I'm your boss, besides I've got work to do. You know, with the book."

"First of all, you aren't my boss, you're my colleague. I write things with you not for you, do I seem like a robot that just punches words into a keyboard?"

"No that's not what I meant, it's just--"

"I know. You can't." Tears growing in her eyes she had to turn away and head for the door.

Ryan would have told her to wait but he just couldn't, he couldn't do a lot of things these days. Move on, keep going. That's what everyone told him to do and it's not like he didn't want to but he didn't know how to move on without feeling like he was leaving everybody else in the past behind. As dark as those memories were, he feared losing touch with them, they were the only thing left that connected him to her. Once they were gone, so was she. Ryan supposed he was in a stage of denial, and that meant that there were only a couple more stages—-at least that's what he thought, he had forgotten what the other stages were but he supposed they would come on naturally.

Breaking his meditative concentration was the loud closing of the front door, Diana was gone and suddenly he could breathe easier. He didn't dislike her, in fact he did have a great admiration for her in many ways, but it felt as if he was trapped in the old world. Reliving his haunting memories night after night, waking in a cold sweat while feeling for his long-gone fingers. He still had the fight or flight mentality, Ryan remembered one night when he was deep in his writing and Diana tapped him on the shoulder to check his progress. He knew it was her, every fiber of his being knew it was her but the touch on his shoulder made him *feel* like it wasn't her. He jumped and knocked over the glass on the table, slicing his arm quite badly in the process. Ever since then Diana didn't question why he couldn't do some things but that didn't mean that she wasn't pained by it.

Moments ago Ryan had wanted her gone, the fear in his chest of coming close to another person was too strong to endure. What if somebody came for her? What would he, could he do? Was it his fault that Becky died? Did it matter?

She was dead.

Ryan felt dead too, an animated corpse.

Someone who cannot protect those he loves, he can't even protect himself.

He wanted her back, not Becky at that moment but Diana. It scared him. It reminded him of when they first met, Becky had been nothing short of amazing in his mind.

Would she want him to live in fear for the rest of his life?

He didn't think so.

Maybe he would die, maybe peacefully, maybe brutally. No matter the cause, one day he would die. He was not going to do it in fear. Ryan felt sadness at the fact that he couldn't be the man he was back when he was with Gareth. When he was tied up, sure of his own death, that was when he had no fear. Now that Ryan was unsure of his death he found himself afraid. Why was that? He decided he would reject it, reject the fear and face his problems. No matter what came next, he would not back down.

He eyed the stress blanket lying on his bed.

Instead Ryan decided to scoop up his landline and start dialing the numbers.

"Yeah, Ron it's me. I'll do the tour."

Then there was a knock at the door.

23

"He's singing."

"And that's bad?"

"He's been singing for fourteen hours."

"Has he stopped at all?"

"No, we tried to bring him water but he hasn't touched any of the cups."

"He needs to start eating, that man hasn't eaten or drank anything since we put him on meds."

"Well that I know but they recommend we keep him on them, at least for the time being."

"And if he doesn't eat?"

"He will, everybody does. Let me have a shot at it."

"Chief, are you sure? The doctor recommended that we don't go in there. Said he's dangerous. I mean not even the guys we got trying to feed him keep their distance."

"I'm sure I'll be fine, I've got a gun at my hip."

"That's what I'm worried about,"

Doors unlocked and Chief Brody walked in as confidently as one could while holding a tray of prison food and a plastic cup filled with water.

He raised his head like someone had woken him from a deep slumber, he mimicked the playing of a trumpet.

"Are we doing okay Gareth?"

Gareth simply whistled.

"Gareth, I asked if we're doing okay."

Gareth continued to sing, "Don't Fence Me In".

"Gareth stop singing."

Darting his head toward her, he stopped.

"Why stop now?" Amelia asked.

"Because you told me to."

"How come you were signing for so long?"

"Nobody told me to stop."

"Well, I've got some food here. We think you should eat this." Amelia said, setting down the tray of food and the cup.

"Thank you."

"You're welcome."

"Do you sing?"

"Do I sing?"

"Yes. Do you sing?"

"Not in a long time."

"Me either, perhaps that's why I sang so long."

"Yeah, maybe." Amelia was getting shivers at how normal of a conversation she was having with an extremely deranged murderer.

"I do love singing. I'd forgotten quite how much."

"Well, that's good. Just make sure you get a bite to eat." Amelia began to get up.

"Gone so soon?"

"I have other business to attend to."

"Did I get a letter today?"

"Who would be sending you letters?"

"This very nice lady named Liv. She has been sending me letters every day and I thought I might have gotten one today. Is there one?"

"Let me check, is that okay?"

"Please check. I hope they didn't lose it in the mail!" Gareth said and chuckled loudly as if he had made a very clever joke.

He continued to stare at Amelia until she flashed a faint grin and closed the door behind her. Gareth remained affixed in this position for a brief few seconds and then folded his hands onto his lap, waiting for Amelia to return with his letter.

As soon as Amelia got out of the room she pursued the officer standing guard at the door.

"Has he been receiving letters?"

"Ye-eah. Um, some girl has been ah—we think it's some sort of fan mail."

"And did you not think that *fan mail* might not be appropriate to give him?"

"There wasn't anything criminal in the letters so we had to waive them through."

"Did he get one today."

"Yeah, one just came in."

"Okay, so he knows what time they usually arrive at. I wanna see it."

24

The tour was nearing its third hour of operation, they took all of the tourists to the locations and then described what had transpired there. Many of the guests were snapping photographs and taking pictures with their loved ones, smiling.

"So where you're standing right now is actually the exact place where Gareth would actually commit some of his murders. In this park he used to frequently slaughter unlucky joggers who just happened to be passing through. You can all continue taking pictures, because we're going to stop here for a few moments so you can really take in the scenery and get some good shots." Tammy the tour guide smiled a hollow desultory smile.

Soon after making her announcement Tammy slithered away to tap on her phone while the guests took action shots of them jumping from the bushes.

From behind her a hand grasped her shoulder, Tammy jumped out of her skin.

"Sorry I didn't mean to startle you," Liv said.

"Oh my, it's quite alright. Sometimes when you're doing these tours the energy of the place gets to you. Don't worry about it. Did you have a question?"

"Yes actually. I did."

"What do you think of the killer?"

"Um…That's a tough question. I'm not usually one to judge anyone but I think what he did and how he did it was particularly disgusting. Did you hear that he kept human organs in jars?"

"Yes actually. I did," Liv said, staring at the guide as if it was rookie knowledge on the subject.

"Oh well, I thought that was very interesting to find out. How sick is that? He said it was like keeping flowers."

"Yeah. I know he did."

"Oh did you read the—"

"Yes I read the book."

"Nice, did you like—"

"Did you know we write letters back and forth, he and I?"

"Is that so?"

"Yes actually."

"Interesting, I think we should um. Probably get going, it's starting to get dark if you've noticed." Tammy checked her watch nervously.

"Yes I have noticed," Liv said and walked away.

Tammy checked her fitness band and it was recording high heart rates, just when she was getting so much progress done with the tour today. Fifty thousand steps and now her heart rate was out of whack.

Perfect, just perfect.

"Okay tour! We're gonna get a move on now, back to our departure location!" Tammy said, she hoped they'd get a move on quickly and not take as many pictures as they did on the way over here.

Taking them to Ryan's old house was a bloody mess, she thought they might even need to remove it from the tour because the new owner who purchased the house was getting rightly pissed off by their presence. Good for them, but Tammy would never be able to live in a house that somebody got murdered in like that, and so soon too.

Hell, they probably got a deal, she thought.

A good deal, she didn't feel too sorry for them.

She was stuck doing serial killer tours with a bunch of weirdos, she did need the money though so she kept her thoughts to herself. Originally the plan was to take them to the stairwell where one of the murders took place, but the hotel owners were not thrilled with the idea and thought it might scare away potential guests. Tammy didn't blame them; she wouldn't want a group of tourists clogging her stairwell talking about how somebody got slashed as people are on their way back to their rooms.

You'd probably get one star for that sort of thing.

Anyhow, they were going back now and when she got home Tammy could draw herself a nice warm bath. That was an encouraging thought. Get home, that's the goal. Not too hard was it? Not when you put it plainly. In reality though, it was a lot harder. Tammy had to physically walk all that way, and when she got to the destination she'd have to come up with some more bullshit about how she enjoyed her time spent with all of them. As if the wind chill didn't freeze her bones to the sidewalk. Still, it paid to let them take their pictures.

That sort of thing got you four and a half stars.

Some folks never did give five stars, maybe the air didn't taste proper enough for them. Who the hell knew, but when you ask someone to give a good rating they start picking out all the flaws in the thing. Tammy was always annoyed that the goal was never to get five stars but to prevent one and two stars. Everyone would go to a three-star tour but under that and your business failed because tours are a dime a dozen and everybody knows where it happened. Today that lady that came up to Tammy got on her nerves, every once in a while, you'd get a smart ass who thinks they know everything and unload all their knowledge on you like they were spies from the company. 'Why don't those people apply for the job and run the tour their damn selves' Tammy thought.

Before she knew it she was one step closer to ending her tour, now it was time for the speech, blah blah blah, this and that, thank you for coming and I enjoyed our time together. Everyone started clapping and that was kind of a silver lining, for a moment she felt like a star. Everybody wants to be the star.

One didn't clap, that girl who approached her earlier. Instead this woman stared at Tammy without a trace of a readable expression. Well who cared anyway, she was about to go home and run her nice warm bath. Forget the woman and just walk home, easy. She'd been walking all day, what were a few more steps?

It was admittedly a lot.

Her rate was through the roof, good thing she was almost home though. Something about that girl frightened her, she had this sense about some people when they looked at you. She could see that behind their eyes there was something off, she could never put a finger on it. That look though, when she got it, it sent something crawling up her spine and then back down again. Tammy saw the look in that girl's eyes, tonight more than most she understood it. It was something broken inside.

In slid the boning knife, deep in her right lung she felt it pierce through. Hollow gasps emanated from her throat as her eyes widened from the shock of it all, she knew it was that fucking girl. Surprisingly enough instead of fear, Tammy felt anger and she tried to snatch the knife from her attacker. Wrestling it from her hands she swiped at Liv and the blade dashed across her palm. Tammy wasn't a stranger to violence, she'd been attacked on the street before while walking home from her tours. She wasn't going down easily. That was until Liv drew a pistol out of her purse and fired all six shots into Tammy's chest. 'What a fucking bitch,' Tammy thought as she died. Meanwhile, that girl just ran off.

Liv loved Gareth, more than most. Liv was surely his number one fan.

25

Ryan answered the door, that was not who he was expecting.

In front of him stood Chief Brody and she wanted to come in, she had some questions.

Ryan thought he had finished answering all of their questions after the incident, although this officer was much kinder about everything.

"I wanna thank you for inviting me in, I know this is a sensitive subject for you and revisiting it I'm sure is painful for you."

"I'm sorry but what did you need?"

"Ah yes, I apologize for the obligatory condolences. I'll get straight to the point. There's been further complications with the case."

"Like what?"

"Well we believe there's a copycat killer on the loose."

"A what?"

"Somebody who mirrors the killings of another murderer."

"No, I know what it is. What do you want with me?"

"Somebody is trying to replicate Gareth's murders. We found a boning knife at the scene of a crime involving a guide of a tour that centered around Gareth."

"Fucking hell...Why...I mean why do you guys need me for this kinda stuff? Aren't you like a cop? Can't you track her down and get her? You can get her like Gareth right?"

"Well, you see it's not that simple. We need evidence. I'm here because we believe you might be a potential target going forward."

"You're kidding."

"As you'd say, I'm afraid I'm not kidding."

"So what do you think this person is gonna try and cut off my fingers? Too bad they're already gone, try again next time. See ya later."

"She sent these photos to Gareth." Amelia laid out several photographs of Ryan and Diana entering and leaving their home.

"What the fuck."

"I understand this may come as a shock to you but—"

"But what, this person knows where I fucking live! Wh-what am I supposed to do? Move! I just bought the fucking place!"

"We were going to recommend you accept police protection for the time being."

"Jesus, that'll help. This psycho killer knows where I live and now I'm gonna have an armed militia outside my door, nice way to live really. Don't know why I didn't think of it before actually."

"I know this isn't ideal but—"

"No thanks."

"I'm sorry?"

"I don't want the help, but thanks."

"Please reconsider what I've asked. Other people could be at stake as well. Anyone you talk to or are in contact with." Amelia noticed as she said this Ryan's face scrunched up, he didn't like the implications of what she just said.

"Okay fine. Put cops outside my door, I doubt I'll sleep easier for it anyway."

"That's good you feel that way, maybe you won't sleep easier but I sure as hell will."

"What are your plans?"

"We've been trying to get Gareth to bring her in for a visit, he refuses to speak with anyone about it though...well..." Amelia's eyes tracked onto Ryan, then averted as if saving him some trouble.

"Well what?"

"He only wants to talk to you, he thinks the two of you are friends."

"Why in the *fuck* would he think that?"

"He has a signed copy of your book where he says you call him 'your best friend'."

"Of course he does."

26

"I'm glad you agreed to do this."

"Did I have another choice? I could live in a fortress all my life or maybe the protection wears off after a while? You see I have to figure this out or I'm dead. It's not like jury duty or something." Ryan took a deep breath and opened the door to see Gareth sitting with his hands folded in his lap.

"Do you have my letter?" Gareth asked before looking up.

"No letters," Ryan said with mustered up courage as he sat across from him.

When Ryan looked up, he saw that Gareth's face lit up with joy.

He clapped his hands and jumped with joy, pointed to Ryan and looked at the police from outside

177

the one-sided window, as if to show them he really came.

"I'm glad you're here Ryan," Said Gareth.

Ryan, while sitting silently, was staring at Gareth—as if he could kill him right there on the spot. Ryan felt like he might be as sick as Gareth at that moment, he was uncomfortable with how easily the feelings came over him.

"I came here for a reason; I'm here to tell you—to tell this girl you've been writing that she should come here and visit you."

"Why would I do that?"

"You said I'm your *best friend* right?"

"You said that. Not me, I'm surprised."

"Why's that?"

"I killed your little girlfriend, no?" As Gareth said this Ryan's chair scratched against the floor, as he shifted his weight in discomfort.

"I upset you, that wasn't my intention. I'm just recalling the facts. There is no reason you should like me and I would understand if you don't. I no longer want to kill anyone. But I have and I'm not sure what to do." Gareth looked off at his feet, as if he was ashamed.

This was truly shocking, Ryan thought he might come here and get mocked but it was the complete opposite. Gareth seemed mournful, guilty. To think the guy that cut off the tips of his fingers felt bad about it, what a world he lived in, our world.

"How come you never killed me?"

"I'm sorry?" Gareth asked, as if he couldn't recall.

"You never killed me; you could have but you kept me around. In a sick way, like a pet. You kept me."

"I um, I...I'm a little embarrassed to be honest. It feels like I'm waking up from a nightmare, but it

179

wasn't a nightmare, and I truly did those horrible things."

"You did. Many, her name was Becky."

"Oh yes, Becky! Where is she?"

"You killed her."

"No, no, no, no, no, no, no." Gareth got up from his seat and started pacing, Ryan heard the door unlock from the outside but put up his hand to indicate he was fine.

"She got in the way. She got in the way; she wasn't supposed to come. You were there with me, we were having a good time. Just us. The two of us were having a good time. We were friends, you were my good friend. Like Phillip. you were...my best friend, my only friend, a good friend, good friend."

"Stop." Ryan said firmly.

"Stop, stop, stop...I can't stop, I won't stop. I can never stop. Art, I need to be an artist. I can't stop until the work is done. Phillip will be angry, I have to finish my work or my book won't come out and I won't be famous and then I'll be sad."

"Phillip? What has he got to do with this?"

"I really shouldn't be saying these things. Friends don't tell on one another."

"You two were friends?"

"Sometimes."

"How does he know you?"

"Helped me with writing, that's all. Nice guy."

"Did he know about what you did?"

"I wasn't fully honest with him, I didn't tell him everything. I just couldn't stop myself."

"You can."

"Help me. I can't, *I can't*."

"I...um...I," Ryan began but couldn't finish.

The words choked up in his throat and wouldn't come up, he wanted to offer his hand. He wanted to offer this poor man his helping hand but he remembered what he'd done with those hands. All those he'd killed, how he butchered Becky like a venison and threw her aside like a hunk of meat. He felt sick suddenly, seeing tears in the eyes of this shaking man across from him that he no longer recognized as a sick murderer but a sick man.

"I will help you," A voice said that was not his own, yet it was his voice.

"You are a good friend."

"No I'm not," Ryan said, and he thought of Becky lying face down while blood poured from her lifeless corpse, no I'm not he thought. No I am not.

"Tell me more about Phillip."

"He said that I would become an artist, I have always wanted to become an artist. Since I was a boy, my mother hated my art. I brought in a dead mouse and she hit me, many times. She said only filthy animals bring in dead things. She never appreciated my art; I didn't want to hurt the mice but I needed what was inside of them to paint. You understand? Don't you?"

182

"Gareth that was not the right thing to do, do you…do you know that now?"

"I don't know, I didn't like them being upset but I needed their parts, my mother told me I didn't deserve the art set I asked for on my birthday because I was *a bad kid*. One day I *really* wanted to paint. I asked her, I said 'mom please I need to paint, I need to become an artist mom, nobody likes me, people like paintings. I *need* to paint for people so someone will like me.' She took the belt and she hit me in my eye, she told me that I am a bastard and no painting will ever make up for the fact that I am a murderer and I kill things. I made her sick but I *needed* to. I had to paint."

"What did you do?"

"Nothing to her, she was too big. *Charlie* wasn't."

"Who is Charlie?" Ryan felt himself getting sick, he didn't want to imagine.

183

"Was."

"Gareth, tell me."

"Charlie was my best friend. He trusted me and I opened him up. That is who Charlie was, I needed his paints. He was a good boy." Gareth began to sob, he fell onto the table and wailed.

"Gareth, it's okay," The words dripped from Ryan's mouth out of habit. In truth he had no idea, none of it sounded okay. He didn't know what to do or say, what was right and what was wrong. Did it matter? Becky was dead either way, what does it matter who's at fault? Maybe it wasn't okay, maybe things aren't always so black and white. Maybe things just were. It didn't matter how you felt about them, so long as you prevented them from happening ever again? Ryan hated Gareth, hated him. He still did. Coming in there he wasn't sure if he would be able to contain himself, now if it were any other person was crying like this he might have hugged him. No, Ryan would never forgive him. Fuck that, he killed so many people. He was a monster but Ryan would never forget the people who *made* him a monster.

"I killed my best friend; I could kill you."

"You don't have to do those things anymore. The people who hurt you are gone. One day you'll learn to live with the things that happened. You'll never forget what you did, but there's still time to try to make it right, maybe you can't. It doesn't matter. Just write to this girl and tell her to come here, tell her to confess. End this."

"I want to, I want to end it. I will write to her and I will end this—for you."

"You're doing a good thing now. You can't change the past but you can always change the future." Ryan got up and strode to the door confidently.

"You truly are a magnificent writer Ryan," Gareth said as Ryan was leaving.

"Thank you."

"No need to thank me, I was only lying. You are a gullible fingerless boy—and you are not the hero, come to save me." Gareth held back a chuckle.

Suddenly it struck him, he saw that face and connected it to the face that killed Becky, he felt like he was going to vomit. Quickly he darted out of the room and the door closed behind him like an echo from another world.

"Is everything alright?" Amelia asked as he fled.

Ryan said nothing.

Quickly he fumbled for his keys as he left in a haze, Chief Brody hurried after him but he ran from her like she was after him.

Ryan got into his car and locked the door; she began to knock against his window.

"You shouldn't drive in this condition Ryan! Turn off the car!" Amelia shouted, Ryan waved his hand at her and tried to drive off, smashing himself into a light post instead.

Blood trickled down his head, he only wished the impact was harder so that he might die. Amelia pulled him from the car and he felt dazed, she sat him up against the light post and began to ask him if he could hear her, he could but he didn't want to.

"I'm awful."

"You're not awful," Amelia assured him.

"I am, he killed her and I was being nice to the fucking guy, that's…that's fucked up."

"Only because you had to, you did a good thing."

"It doesn't feel like I did a *good thing*."

"It shouldn't feel like it, but it is."

"Does he even deserve help?"

"Probably not, no."

"So many other people die because of him so why is *he* the one who should get my help?"

187

"Here's how I look at it, I've been on this job for a long time and I've seen a lot of fucked up shit. I find a person and they've just killed somebody, should I kill them? Is that going to bring back the person they killed? I say no, and why should I create more of the stuff?" Amelia looked off into the distance. "I try not to think about it all until it's done. Then I figure it all out afterwards, could I have done it better? Usually the answer is no. Try and look at it from my perspective, would you expect any normal person to deal with all this? I don't think so. So why do you expect it of yourself?"

"Because I'm all that's left. I feel like I owe it to them to fix things."

"You don't *owe* them anything. You didn't do anything to them. It's not your fault, you gotta stop beating yourself up."

"I'll try not to."

"You know what? Why don't I give you a ride home?" Amelia looked over to the totaled car, "I think you'll need one."

27

"Really it's not that bad."

"It looks pretty fucking bad."

"It's just a couple scratches, trust me; the pictures look worse than it actually is. Just gonna have to send the car into the shop is all."

"I'm worried about you, not the car."

"Oh, well I'm fine and I'm pretty sure you don't even need a bumper to drive anyways."

"Okay well, just be careful and get home safe," Diana said and hung up, as if it would make Ryan safer to end the call earlier. He found it funny that she called it 'home' as if it was both of theirs. He'd invited her over tonight to 'talk' so he was expected tonight to be tough, keep in mind that one night he had all his fingers cut off below the second knuckle. Emotions were always harder, beforehand. Physical pain was

190

almost always worse in the moment, time would always make it feel distant and not as bad. Until you felt it again.

But now he wasn't feeling it, he was feeling butterflies in his stomach because he had to talk to a girl, not just any girl but *her*. If ever you feel like the world has ended just remember that eventually, with time, you will be able to worry yourself over nothing once again.

When he entered, Ryan found that the door to the house closed louder than he remembered it being able to close, did they mess with the door? Hopefully they didn't, because he just painted it. Honestly, he shouldn't have even let them lurk around his home like this and—oh, there she is.

Diana was standing at the top of the stairs waiting for him, it'd been another long night and he promised to be home earlier tonight but…what did he even have to apologize for? They weren't married,

191

Ryan thought. Still, he wouldn't dare say something like that.

"Late again?"

"Can I say no?"

"If you want to sleep in the rain, they're calling for a thunderstorm."

"Hold up, you can't kick me out of my own house."

Diana danced down the stairs and pressed a finger into his chest.

"Don't test me, I could *fuck* you up—" She couldn't contain her laughter and began to wheeze out like a stepped onto a dog's toy.

"Oh is that so?"

"Yup." Diana lightly punched him in the shoulder.

Pretending to be hurt, Ryan dropped to the floor as if he'd been knocked out, he fell in slow motion, like they did in boxing films. She roared with laughter and couldn't breathe as she snickered at his tragic fall.

"Oh no, you've been killed! Let me take you back to my *lair*. Ha-ha, ha-ha-ha!"

Ryan tugged back his foot and stood himself upright, before he said anything, Diana already knew what she'd done.

"I'm so sorry, I didn't even think of it."

"It's okay, don't worry about it. I'm not made of glass; I just think we should get working while it isn't too late."

Why did she have to say that? Of all the things, why did joking about killing your friends have to be such a common way to poke fun? Diana knew she'd hurt him tonight, it was an awful thing to happen because it couldn't be undone, it was immutable.

It was hard for social situations to regain their equilibrium after being knocked out of balance by a pinch of awkwardness. Once the energy was lost it was as frivolous as the pursuit of nostalgia to try and regain it. She had hoped they could talk things over tonight and maybe even she could tell him how she was feeling but now it just...didn't feel right.

"I need to finish this book, but I just can't get it right."

"Well, if you can't do it right then wait."

"Until when?"

"There's no time limit until when, you'll just know. The idea will come and then just write it down. I know you have other ideas but then you wait and you lose those ones waiting for these ones that aren't ready yet."

"But this is my *best* work."

"*Your* best work? You were co-writing it and now that she's—"

"What? Now that she's dead I can't finish it?"

"That's not what I was saying."

"You were about to."

"If I was going to say then I'd have said it. What I meant is that she's not going to hate you because you can't finish your book together."

"You're right, because she's dead. And that…That sicko killed her, now apparently I'm his best buddy and I've got to deal with all of his fucking problems! How the fuck is that fair?"

"It's not fair, it just is."

"That doesn't help."

"Well I can't help you."

"Then what's the point in talking?"

"I'm not saying you shouldn't talk but I can't change the way things are, believe me I would. If for anyone in the world I would change things they'd be for you."

"I'm…sorry. This is just—"

"You don't need to apologize, I understand."

"People think that if you acknowledge that you understand why somebody is being an asshole then it makes them stop being an asshole. So I understand that you understand but I'm sorry, I'm not going to unload on you because I can't keep all my shit packed up inside."

"You don't need to, you just need to remember that I'm on your side."

"I know you are. Sometimes I just yell and then I get even more angry that I'm yelling at you and I yell more which seems counterintuitive but really it should—"

"Do you want to be with me?" Diana asked despite herself.

"Uh…"

"Okay." Diana grabbed her backpack and began to pack up her stuff.

"Stop."

"I want to." Tears were growing in her eyes.

"Please, I want you to stay but I don't know how to say it."

"You just said it."

Diana's last teardrop landed on the carpet below.

28

"Thank you everyone for coming today, I realize some of you had to wait out in the rain and I thank you all for your patience," Ryan said, although he was kind of annoyed that the rain didn't send them home, it meant he was probably in for some of the loopier fans today. This was bound to be fun.

Ever since Ryan's book was released, people have been trying to find copies of Gareth's version of *The Killing Stroke* novel online. Somehow it got leaked, not everyone on the force is Brody. People were paying upwards of five hundred dollars per copy, many copies were being sold with 'original autographs' from Gareth himself.

The things people spend their money on.

Who was he to speak in the first place? He was the one allowing people to spend their money on *his* book. Just because it was another more terrible person telling the story did not mean that they were telling a different story, same story, same profits. One silver lining Ryan could find was that at the very least you could see this story through the eyes of an appropriate narrator. Yet even that wasn't wholly true, there were so many cooks in the kitchen that the book that came out wasn't quite the book he wrote. All of the touching emotional tribute to victims he wrote were replaced with thrilling descriptions of the murders that he didn't even write. Of course Ryan was astounded by these changes, especially considering that it looked like many of the gory parts were directly lifted from *The Killing Stroke*. At the end of the day Ryan didn't know what he found more disturbing, the fact that they took from a book that was written in league with a murderer or that people accused Ryan's book of plagiarising from it, as if *they* were the bad guys. Ryan would have, should have objected to the changes, but truth be told...He couldn't afford to.

Here they came one again, it felt like going to work. He thought he'd found a loophole in becoming an author, you have a good enough story and somebody will write it *for* you. It wouldn't have been all too bad of a life if it didn't require such a high price to be paid for it. He liked not having to do much, but truth be told, there was no such thing as a job with no strings attached. You always had to answer somebody's email and go to somebody's press event. That is to say, if you want to profit off of the public, you better be prepared to deal with them when you do.

"Hi, can you make it out to Billy?"

"Yeah um, sure I can." Ryan could feel himself zoning out.

"It's for his birthday, teenagers and the things they ask for. Am I right?"

Ryan didn't notice his blank expression until the woman's face soured and he realized he was being rude "Oh..haha. Yeah," was all he said.

"He just loves horror! I'm sure he's gonna love it."

"You know this book is pretty graphic right?"

"Oh I know, but I tell him as long as you don't do that stuff then it's okay."

"Yeah, alright. Ok." Ryan handed back the book, it was going to be a long day.

Later he'd have to have another therapy session with that psycho while he waited for his secret admirer to show up.

He couldn't believe he was going back.

When he got there, the prison grounds were covered in a thick morning fog, the rain died down to a trickle but it was forecasted to come down hard later tonight again. Ryan really didn't give a fuck about the rain, he was about to go back into that room with that man. He told himself it didn't bother him to think about it and in his head it didn't. Once he was about to say his name or talk about the events Ryan found that he always danced around the story that read so clearly in his thoughts. He always felt he was having a nightmare when he stepped into that room with that thing. Until it started to speak.

"Hello Ryan."

"How are you?" He couldn't believe he was asking this.

"I am well, yourself?" Gareth asked, great Ryan thought. Small talk.

"Yeah, um I'm fine. Listen, did you send that girl the letter?"

"Yes, but do not be surprised if she does not come today."

"Why wouldn't she come?"

"I suspect that she is suspicious of my invitation." Gareth's leg shook as he spoke.

"What would she suspect?"

"I am not sure to be quite honest. I tried to speak as if nothing was amiss. Although we have already established our delight in keeping the contact in pen alone. This way there would be nobody to suspect what she—I have said more than I intended and I apologize for cutting myself off."

"I'm interested in what you have to say."

"I am sure you are Ryan."

"What would people suspect of her?"

"Please do not ask."

"If she's done something, something *terrible*. You can tell me."

"Can I tell you Ryan? Can I."

"You can."

"True, I could. But we are not alone." Gareth smiled.

Ryan sat with his hands folded on the table, they were not alone.

That was actually a relief.

"Nothing to say? For such a great writer I would expect you would have more to say. Nonetheless I do." Gareth sat back in his chair, commanding control of the room. "If I tell you anything, they will find her. Then they put her in a room just like this one, I do not support the unjust incarceration of artists. When the public hears my story, I will be released and you will be sorry for treating me in this way."

"You belong here. You know that."

"Sure, I will think whatever they want me to when they clip my wings. Now I know where I belong, I am not stupid."

"You're right where you belong."

"That is where you are wrong. Soon enough I will get back to my butchering and saucy creations."

"What kind of monster are you?"

"Monster! That is rich. And here I thought we were friends."

"Don't you dare."

"You see, your pity is conditional. So long as I am beneath you and do not challenge you, you will for my well being. As if I am this poor sick animal limping at your doorstep. *Please, oh please Ryan nurse me back to health! Only you are capable!* What sort of story did you think this was? This is your story, now you are supposed to forgive me and start over happy and new. You see through the eyes of a writer, thinking there is a story under all the blood and bones but there is not. If there is any story at all, It is mine."

"No it's not."

"One thing is for sure; it is not Becky's story. Maybe it is Diana's. Do you think?"

That's when he hit him, the first time.

He didn't remember stopping but they pulled him off of Gareth when they rushed into the room.

205

He'd already done enough damage by the time they got in, his prosthetics cut deep. Gareth was blinking through the blood that was pouring out of his nose and down the back of his neck. It had been a long time since he felt the feel of his own blood, it was usually others.

"You see, we are not so different after all. I am sure they can find room for you next door." Gareth began to laugh a sick gargled laugh.

Outside of the room, Ryan came face to face with Amelia.

"I'm gonna look the other way and pretend I didn't see that on account of your—"

"No, you're gonna tell me what the fuck is going on."

"You jumped on him and started to attack him."

"Don't give me that shit, how's it gonna look on you if someone you chose to involve in an investigation went loose on a patient here. I'm not a cop or anything but I don't think it's a good look on you."

"It's gonna be hard to explain."

"Figure it out, that's not my problem."

"It could be."

"I know you'll figure something out." Ryan smiled a cocky smile that he might have given before everything had happened, it chilled him how much we reverted to our regular selves when under pressure.

Ryan stopped dead in his tracks and turned to Amelia, "She's not coming anyways so you can— *Diana*." Ryan's blood ran cold.

That's why the admirer wasn't coming. How could Gareth know her name?

"Can you give me a ride?"

"Is everything alright?" Amelia asked.

"I'm not sure but we need to hurry."

29

Diana had arrived early and let herself in with the key, she was freshening up in the washroom when she entered the home. The officers stationed outside of the house were changing shifts, but Liv already knew that. It was getting late, usually Ryan would be home by now and they would start brainstorming the reasons why he was unable to come up with the next chapter of whatever he was working on. Usually the project would be shelved because 'he'd run out of ideas'. Still, that didn't stop Diana from pursuing his inspiration to wherever it might lead. Now it was about to lead her somewhere quite perilous.

That's when she heard the steps.

"Do you need anything?" Diana asked, to whom she assumed to be an officer.

No answer was returned to her. She *knew* it was a cop, but she was afraid it was that killer they'd talked about. This was ridiculous, she'd already discussed her flaws at length on how she inflates every little thing to mean the end of the—

Bullets ripped through the fresh white paint on the door. Diana screamed; her neck was bleeding. It wasn't too deep but it was surely bleeding badly, she moved away from the doorframe and got to cover in the bathtub. She yanked at all the toilet paper and used it to cover her neck which was shooting blood. Diana heard weak kicks strike the door, then somebody was throwing their weight against the door as hard as they could.

They weren't too heavy.

It still wasn't over, she'd need to be ready. Diana launched herself out of the tub, slick with blood and quickly shot her arm past the door frame and yanked her wash-bag off of the counter beside her. She was feeling dizzy and knocked her head against the porcelain toilet beside the bath while looking for some sort of weapon.

She only found a small travel sized pair of scissors.

Trying to get up was difficult because of how slippery the blood had made everything. She was sliding around as if she was trying to steady herself on a smooth sheet of moss.

Diana got to the door and fell with a thud.

Gunshots again, the door handle fell limply out of place, dangling like a broken wrist.

Coming into the bathroom was a woman brandishing a boning knife and a gun, Diana only saw a flash of her ankle but that was all she needed. Liv didn't see her because she was on the floor, but she assumed her job was done when she saw all the blood, she didn't see the pair of scissors about to be lodged into her ankle though.

It sounded like a shriek, the woman who Diana saw fell onto her back and tried to run. Liv placed her hands on the doorframe and pulled herself out of the bathroom, she screamed now. Diana assumed she was trying to get the scissors out from her ankle, it was a good stab.

'What kind of hack-job killer gets stabbed by their own victim?' she thought.

Liv heard the officers coming up the stairs and she left the way she came, dropped herself out the window. Diana heard another yelp after Liv's crash into the bushes below. When the police downstairs arrived, they were more concerned with attending to her wounds than pursuing the assailant. She was thankful for that, but at the same time she wished she had the strength to pursue the bitch herself. Diana wasn't one to sleep easy with someone after her head, she wanted this thing put to bed. They sent one cop to go after Liv, but by the time they did that she was long

gone. Probably crafting another love letter.

30

When they arrived other squad cars were already on the scene, Ryan blasted out of the car and ran upstairs to see her. She was lying in bed resting and the sheets were a bloody mess.

"I'm sorry about the sheets."

"Fuck the sheets, are you okay?"

"Yeah I just got shot in the neck. It's not that bad really." She began to giggle.

"Now's not the time to make fun of me."

"Isn't it? I'm pretty sure the injured person always gets to decide what's funny."

"Not when I'm injured."

"Fair enough."

"You just get some rest okay. I'll get those sheets changed for you in a minute," Ryan said and quietly exited the room, he was about to close the door but Diana told him she'd feel safer with it open.

He hated to see her become like him. She looked afraid. When he first met her he didn't exactly like how she didn't seem to understand the reality of the world. Ryan realized then that the reason he was upset with her attitude was that he was jealous of it. He couldn't let her lose that defiant optimism, he wouldn't.

Ryan hurried down the stairs, at the bottom he caught a glance of Amelia in the middle of discussion with her surrounding officers. Something seemed to be urgent, characters were clearing out of the estate with haste. Ryan crossed into the eyeshot of Amelia and he caught her gaze, pulling her from the spell engaged conversation cast upon you.

"She's there now," Brody said.

She didn't wait for an answer.

"You coming?" Brody asked.

31

"Are you happy to see me?"

"I am overjoyed." Gareth made an attempt at a smile.

The discomfort read plain on Liv's face; she gave an uncomfortable smile back.

"I've been waiting for this moment for so long, you're my hero."

"I am glad."

"You know, I've been doing some *art* myself."

"That's good. Would you like to tell me about it?"

"In…In *here*?"

"Are you afraid to speak your mind here?"

"No, I'm not afraid it's just…"

"Then tell me what you've done."

"I used…"

"Go on now, we're waiting."

"Well, I tried to use a boning knife but…I had to shoot her. It was still beautiful to watch the blood spray across the sidewalk."

"You are proud of this?"

"Um I-I thought you'd be happy."

"*Happy*? Do you realize how serious what you have done is? You've committed…Plagiarism."

"I'm sorry darling, how can I do better next time? I wanna be your woman still."

"Next time don't steal somebody else's work! Have you no shame?"

"Please don't yell sweetheart."

"Do you know how hard I worked to make that book? What sacrifices I made!"

"I know."

"You don't know! I am in this prison because I wanted the world to see my art!"

"Someday you'll get out and we'll be together forever babe."

"I have three life sentences you fucking imbecile!"

"We'll get a lawyer and we can—"

"Can I tell you something?"

"Anything darling." Never before had Gareth cringed at something.

"I did not take my medication today."

"Why?"

"So that I could do this."

Gareth sprung to his feet and wrapped his hands around Liv's throat. He was going to end this, like he *promised*. Then the guards burst in.

"Stop! Now!" One of them yelled.

So he did, the guard put his knee onto his back and pressed Gareth against the concrete floor.

"Get his gun," Gareth told her.

Liv snatched the weapon from his hand.

"Point it at him," Gareth instructed.

"Now give it to me," He told her, holding his hand out.

From down the hall Ryan and Amelia heard it go off. When they got to the room they saw the mess, brains splattered on the floor, a limp corpse staring out with fish-like eyes.

Liv didn't expect those bullets to punch holes in her, poor thing. She thought she was handing the gun over to a lover, but she was just another piece of meat. There was no sign of the guard, but it was clear that Gareth had taken him.

The pair had made their way outside where they saw several prison guards with their rifles laid across the pavement with their hands on their heads. Across the yard, Gareth sat in the passenger seat of a squad car, he had the guard at the steering wheel—and he made sure to wave goodbye as he forced them to drive off at gunpoint.

"Goodbye!" Gareth shouted back to them, he smiled at Ryan.

32

In a couple days they found the body. The officer was left in the sweltering heat with his brains imploded all over the steering wheel. Another officer opened the squad car door and the stench hit him at once, he almost wretched. Brody gripped him by the shoulder and held him steady.

"In what world is that *art*?" The officer asked.

"Not ours," Brody said.

"Fucking hell. I'm gonna need to sit down."

"Take all the time you need." Brody dismissed the officer for the moment.

Around the back of the squad car Brody began to conduct a circle check for any more potential evidence. Nothing left behind. She made her way to the front, felt the hood, still hot. Somebody had called in some gunshots in the area, Amelia knew what had happened before they arrived on scene. Ryan was waiting in the back of her own squad car, shouting over to her with a myriad of questions she tried to ignore while looking around. Gareth left the vehicle parked on the side of a highway, good thing they got there before some poor driver just looking to help-out.

Brody was grasping at straws, she couldn't think of where he could have gone, they'd just have to wait and hope the bastard got sloppy again. The thought of that made her sick. They'd just have to wait until he killed some more people. They couldn't, yet what else was there to trace? They couldn't just rely on more anonymous calls to come in. Unless they weren't anonymous.

Amelia rushed back to her squad car and asked Ryan, "Do you know anyone named Phillip Fairview?"

"Yeah, why?"

"Do you know where he lives?"

"Just up Crystal Street, what's going on?"

221

"I think he knows him better than he lets on. Not to mention that book of his, I went through it, and I think he wrote it for him."

"You can't be fucking serious."

"I am, the similarities to the cases were unsettling, so much so that a case was opened against Phillip. He's been under investigation since Gareth's arrest."

"And how come I wasn't informed?"

"You're a civilian. Besides, it had nothing to do with you."

Ryan jumped out of the backseat "Nothing to do with me? You're kidding!"

"Just calm down, okay? I'm gonna have a conversation with the other officers so we can figure out what we're gonna do. I need you to wait here and calm down in the meantime."

"Yeah, sure. I'll calm down," Ryan said.

Brody turned her back and in an instant she heard the police cruiser rip away with it's lights flashing, Ryan was in the driver's seat. Why the fuck had she left the keys in the car? *I'll be surprised if I'm still the chief after this one*, she thought.

33

Phillip unlocked his front door and slid into his house on his socks after removing his shoes. The man flew up his stairs and when he got to his bedroom he flicked on another Sinatra song, this time he chose "My Way", and had it play on his enormous sound system. Roaring vibrations rumbled through his home, when the song had ended he fell back and sprawled along his bed; resting his arms across the fabulous linen he exhaled a sigh of relief.

He'd done it, he'd actually done it.

Sliding between his ribcage was the boning knife that Gareth had pushed into his lung, he'd done it as well. What a fool, he'd thought Gareth could just be done away with so easily and that was the end of it? Ha! He'd have never let it go so easily and Phillip should have known, that fool; now it was time for

Gareth to write the ending to *his* novel, this was going to be good.

Enshrouded in shadow, untouched by the lamplight at the edge of Phillip's bed stood Gareth. There he was dancing to the next song that came on, another Sinatra, "I've Got You Under My Skin".

"Oh Phillip, this is quite ironic don't you think? I remember once you told me that taking the breath away from someone and making them unable to scream for help was actually not terrifying. Well is it? You should know by now. No, don't speak. I can see it in your eyes," Gareth said while Phillip thrashed around on his bed, flailing helplessly. "Stop that you're making a mess you old fool, look at me Phillip and stop that! It's over now." Gareth grabbed Philip's bloody face, forcing him to look into his eyes. "You should have known, now come here, I'm going to finish my book." Gareth threw him further up onto the bed, knocking a violent wheeze from his chest.

Gareth yanked a pen from his own shirt pocket and flipped to the back of the book.

"I always wondered why they left blank pages at the end, well now we'll make use of them, won't we? Won't we!" Gareth shouted, kicking Phillip in his overgrown gut and began to write…

'Gareth had followed him home, slid in through the gate before it closed and followed closely behind, catching the door before it shut. After all was thought to be said and done, Gareth appeared in the bedroom of the famous writer, the true hero of the story had come to settle the score. Phillip had lied, Gareth thought they were friends—but never mind that now, everyone would now know the truth. That this book was not fictitious and indeed was not just *based* on a true story. It *was* a true story. It was *my* story and I hope you enjoyed it. Yours truly, Gareth.' He wrote with a smile.

"There! I have signed it," Gareth announced. "Now it will be worth something someday, give it to one of your fans!" Gareth tossed the book at Phillip's wavering head.

"There you go, you useless spit, oh and I will sign my unaltered version as well, we can leave that for the police to find with you, this will all get out and you will be unanimously hated. Meanwhile all my true fans will adore me. Goodbye Phillip, I wish I could say it was a pleasure," Gareth said, leaving him to die on his fine silk sheets.

Behind him there he was. Ryan creaked open the door to find the horrific scene before him, he saw Phillip's limp corpse staring at him with marble eyes. Gareth turned himself to face him and smiled even wider, brandishing his glimmering blade. Blood was everywhere, pouring from Phillip's chest like a fountain.

"A sight for sore eyes," Gareth laughed.

Ryan dashed at Gareth to wrestle the knife from his hands, he couldn't feel the blade due to the prosthetics. Thrusting downwards, Gareth was attempting to push the knife into Ryan's chest but before he could—Ryan fell backward onto the bed and into the blood pool Phillip was producing. This ripped the blankets off the bed and Phillip's dead husk slid off with them, hitting the carpet with a wet thunk.

Ryan hurled a lamp at Gareth and it broke on his shoulder.

"You are making this harder than it needs to be," Gareth said.

Ryan tried to take a step back but slipped on the blood spreading beneath him—onto his back again, Gareth readied himself for another strike, Ryan tried to get up but continued to slip on the blood which he was now covered with.

"This is it." Gareth smiled.

Ryan yanked the carpet out from under Gareth and he fell hard, dropping his knife. It fell with a clatter and the two scrambled to get a hold of it, Ryan pulled at Gareth's leg but his prosthetic fingers lost grip. Gareth snatched up the knife and shook it free of blood—thrusting it at Ryan, catching him in the flank.

In shock, Ryan's eyes opened wide. Then the adrenaline kicked in.

He threw an elbow into Gareth's chin, knocking some of his teeth through the air. Blood was seeping out of his side, but Ryan kept feeding Gareth elbows to the face.

Gareth pushed him off and made an attempt to get up—but slipped on the blood and hit his face off of the bed frame, breaking his nose.

Ryan kicked him in the face, falling in the process.

Gareth's face knocked against the bed frame more violently than before and shattered the rest of his

229

teeth. Stumbling backward, Gareth fell onto Phillip's gelatinous body.

In the blood and scattered teeth Gareth writhed while to regain his footing.

Meanwhile Ryan was standing with a wobble, he pulled the blade from his body and dropped it to the ground with a dainty splash.

Gareth tried to pull himself up with the nightstand and ended up whipping the landline handset into his head. The entire nightstand tipped over onto him and the cheap wood broke into splinters.

Ryan tackled him, Gareth gripped his throat and made a weak effort to throttle him. Ryan then started throwing heavy jabs at him with his metal prosthetics—which cut Gareth's face in horrendous fashion. Ryan continued to punch Gareth until his grip on his throat loosened.

Gareth fell backwards like a ragdoll. Ryan stood up—but was unable to stay up, falling back onto the carpet near our late Philip, he pressed his hand against the man's cold face and pushed his beady eyes away from him. Ryan was holding his side to keep the blood all packed in. Up above he watched the ceiling fan spin, around and around, around and around, around and—

Amelia bursted in through the front door, behind her was the entire town's police force. They converged on the scene and entered behind her, she rushed up the stairs and set eyes upon the carnage. Ryan was lying in a comatose state with his head cocked in her direction.

She checked for a pulse.

"He's breathing, let's get him in an ambulance!" Amelia shouted, Ryan met her eyes and started to get up.

"No, no. You stay still. I need you to stay still, okay?"

Ryan resisted. "Diana's waiting, she's at home."

"I know, just sit tight. You'll be home soon."

"Thank god, I'm so tired."

Amelia helped the paramedic team get him onto the stretcher, he kept clinging to her uniform and trying to walk.

"You gotta go with them, alright?" Amelia told him.

"Alright." Ryan said but kept trying to walk unaided.

"No. Stop, lie down."

"Okay, am I going home?"

"Yeah, you'll get there."

"Alright, then I'm going to bed." Ryan closed his eyes.

"No, you can't go to bed. You gotta stay awake."

"Okay but how long?"

232

"Until you're at home."

"Okay."

"Deal?" Amelia held onto his hand like a vice-grip to accentuate how serious she was.

"Okay, deal." Ryan gave her a thumbs up, but replaced his hand when he noticed some extra blood pouring out.

"Sounds good. You get yourself home, alright?" Amelia let go of his hand and gave him a tap on the shoulder as the paramedics took him away.

She immediately saw to the rest of the scene, Phillip was lifelessly sprawled across the carpet and Gareth was dry heaving with his back against the wall. Amelia carefully approached him with her gun drawn, although Gareth just tipped over like an empty medicine bottle—he collapsed onto his side and spat up a clump of blood, along some tooth fragments.

Amelia sheathed her pistol and strapped the handcuffs onto the suspect.

Gareth didn't resist, he sat and swayed,

coughing specks of blood here and there.

Looking at his pathetic state Amelia almost

pitied him, but not quite. She knew what he'd done and

responded to some of his grisliest work. There wasn't

an ounce of sympathy in her heart for that man. Just a

cold dark cell waiting for him back at the precinct.

34

"Honey, how are you feeling?" Diana asked while chopping some onions.

"Better, a lot better," Ryan said.

"I'm glad that you took some time to process this. I'm proud of you."

"Thanks, I'm glad I finally listened to you for once. I know I'll never get it out of my head but it doesn't mean I've got to focus on it all the time. I like how you said it was like getting spam mail, just because you get it doesn't mean you need to open it."

"You know what we went through was extremely fucked up, it's okay for you to not be fully okay. You don't have to pretend for me anymore."

"I know. I'm not pretending."

"I just know how you don't like to let me know how you're feeling sometimes."

"Right now, I'm feeling lucky."

"*Lucky?*" Diana asked, her eyebrows jumped and she stopped cutting her onions.

"Yeah, I am lucky. I made it, others didn't. I need to always remember how lucky I am just for being alive another day. This is a gift, it's a gift to spend the rest of my life with you. I'm lucky to have found someone else who gives me a reason to wake up in the morning. I'm lucky," Ryan said, and Diana began to cry.

"These onions are really getting to me," She joshed, cleaning off her blade with a dish towel.

"I mean it."

"I know you do; you didn't think I meant I was crying from the onions, did you?" Diana laughed.

"Ladies and gentlemen, here is your encore, the one the only...Eddie Murphy!"

That got him another pillow to the head.

"So, what's next for us? Should we—I dunno write about it all now?"

"Not this time, I've got another idea in mind."

"Her book idea?"

"No, I was thinking of writing our own book."

Epilogue

It had been months of the same, Gareth woke up and would stare at the same chip in the wall he had all the days before. He'd grown a hefty beard across his face, which made it hard to see his broken up teeth when he spoke. Words didn't quite sound right and came out all jumbled, if he spoke at all. The man barely ate and wouldn't quite look at anyone who interacted with him, just kept staring at that chip in the wall.

Today Gareth was staring at the chip and realized something he'd known all along. That this part of the room was the best part. The chip wasn't supposed to happen, but it did and the wall couldn't be unchipped.

In came the camera crew, Gareth looked in their direction confused.

"Hello Gareth, I'm with Webflix and we were wondering if you would be interested in participating in a documentary series we're producing. It comes out this summer and people are going to just *love* it."

Gareth smiled. "They always do."

28213073R00141